FROM THE ASHES

BERLIN FRACTURED, BOOK 1

MARION KUMMEROW

From the Ashes

Berlin Fractured Series, Book 1

Marion Kummerow

ISBN Paperback: 978-3-948865-25-2

All Rights Reserved

Copyright © 2019 Marion Kummerow

Cover Design by JD Smith Design

Cover photo: Bundesarchiv, Bild 183-M1203-329 / CC-BY-SA 3.0

https://creativecommons.org/licenses/by-sa/3.0/de/deed.en

CONTENTS

CHAPTER 1

Berlin, May 1945

The Ilyushin aircraft hummed through the air and it didn't take long for Werner Böhm to nod off. At long last he was on his way back to Berlin. Memories streamed into his mind, happy ones and not so happy ones.

"Look at these ruins." The voice of his superior, Norbert Gentner, startled him.

Werner opened his eyes and leaned forward to look out of the tiny window. He drew in a shocked breath. Even though he'd anticipated rubble and destruction, he hadn't been prepared for the utter devastation he saw. Miles and miles of nothing but smoldering ruins lay beneath the aircraft. He felt a tug at his heartstrings. Berlin had once – a lifetime ago – been his home.

"Our Red Army certainly hasn't left many reminders of Hitler's fascist regime," he said, wise enough not to mention that the British and American bombers had been responsible for most of the destruction and the Great Red Army had only razed to the ground what was already crumbling.

Gentner, a man in his forties with a balding head and a goatee beard, nodded. "Yes, our army has done a stellar job and we can't praise Stalin enough for his foresight to be the first ones to reach the defeated capital. You'll soon witness how this will help us to implement a demilitarized democracy after the Russian model. It's not often that you get the opportunity to build an entire country from a blank slate."

"I feel very honored to be part of your group, Comrade Norbert," Werner said.

Norbert Gentner was the head of a delegation of German émigrés in Moscow assembled by Stalin to rebuild Berlin according to his wishes. A member of the communist KPD party, Gentner had fled the Nazis in 1938 and arrived in Moscow three years later after stations in Paris and Prague. Since then he'd been trained to take over the government of a defeated Germany. It was an exceptional honor to be selected as part of Gentner's "shadow cabinet" that would take Germany's future in its hand. It was Werner's chance to make history.

At the age of twenty-eight German-born Werner had lived longer in Russia than in his home country. For the past fifteen years he'd worked relentlessly to be in the position he now had, and he vowed not to ruin this fantastic opportunity. He had so many suggestions for improvement of the existing socialism in Russia and itched to discuss some of his theories with Norbert.

"It won't be an easy task, though." Norbert observed the younger man through his spectacles and Werner felt suddenly inadequate. Despite his education at the Moscow University he could never measure up to his icon, who was a well-travelled and distinguished man whom Werner had looked up to since his childhood. The older man's wisdom and accumulated experience were legendary.

"We have to undo twelve years of Nazi brainwashing and re-educate the people in the anti-fascist sense," Norbert said.

"Yes, Comrade, I'm aware of this and I feel well prepared for such a monumental task." Werner studied Norbert's face. He looked serious and exhausted.

"I'm sure, you have studied the theories. But what we face here is the reality," Norbert said. Werner nodded, not daring to interrupt his boss. "Comrade Stalin wishes us to build a demilitarized democratic state. But what might seem easy, won't be. It is a Herculean task for us to accomplish and we need everyone to pull at the rope. The German people have been thoroughly corrupted by fascism and we must be on guard at all times. We cannot indulge them, nor can we become soft. Instead we need to look out for signs of reversion into fascism and eradicate this evil without mercy."

Werner had heard these exact sentences a thousand times during his formative years in the Komsomol and at Moscow University. His admiration for Gentner was evaporating fast. His icon did not live up to his reputation. Throughout the entire journey from Moscow to Berlin the man had shown himself to be a zealous party official who rehashed every officially approved directive, never once changing as much as a single comma.

"I agree, Comrade, fascism is the evil we must obliterate, but surely that will work better if we gain the trust and friendship of the Germans first," Werner said.

Gentner pushed up his spectacles on his nose. "That is a nice little theory. In reality, the German responds best to orders." He leaned back, glancing out of the window and then turned his attention toward Werner again. "I don't fault you for your romantic ideas, because you were too young to understand what happened before Hitler's coming to power. Fascism didn't start with the *Machtübernahme*, its seeds had been planted long before. Under my guidance, I'm sure you will become a very valuable party official."

Werner felt the sting of Norbert's arrogance, and he didn't think he needed guidance if that consisted exclusively in official party wisdom or Stalin quotes. He had probably studied Leninism and Marxism far more intensively than the older man.

All these years in school and university, discussing the benefits of communism, had equipped him with the intellectual weapons to beat anyone in a political argument. Which he suspected was the main reason why he'd been chosen to become Gentner's right hand: because Werner wielded the power of the word like nobody else did.

"I am more than eager to learn from your vast real-life experiences," he said, enthusiastically. It wouldn't do his career any good to give the slightest impression of disloyalty. Norbert might have lost all connection with the reality he so much liked to mention, or the gift of independent thinking, but he was in Stalin's good graces and the designated chairman of the German KPD, tasked with manning the new self-governing structures in Berlin. If Werner aspired to a political career, it was at Norbert's side.

The aircraft jumped and moments later the pilot announced the imminent landing at the airport. Werner fastened the seatbelt and leaned back in his seat, swallowing down the rising malaise from the jumpy ride. Thankfully, the pilot brought the aircraft down safely without too much of a bump when the wheels hit the rough landing strip.

"Welcome to Berlin," the pilot announced.

Werner waited until Norbert gathered up his briefcase and

then helped him into his greatcoat, before he put on his own. It didn't take long for the ten-man delegation to disembark and step onto German soil.

He had last seen the capital as a ten-year-old boy in 1927, when his communist parents had emigrated to Russia, and his heart filled with nostalgia. He inhaled deeply, expecting the air to smell fresh and woody, the way he remembered it. Instead, he scrunched his nose at the intense odor of smoldering heat.

A cough followed his first breath and he scanned the surroundings. Columns of black smoke stood against the horizon, thick and solid, the acrid scent lingering in the air. It was a distinct and disgusting smell, not only of burning wood, but also of incinerated flesh. The delegation hurried to cross the patchy airstrip and boarded the waiting cars. After a bumpy ride past more rubble than Werner had ever imagined existed, the delegation reached their headquarters in the Prinzenallee in Berlin-Lichtenberg.

A smartly dressed soldier greeted them and showed them the spacious modern building that betrayed little war damage. The apartments on the ground floor had been converted into offices and each of the ten men was assigned quarters in one of the higher-up floors to live in.

Werner hadn't even had the time to unpack his suitcase when someone knocked at the door.

"Yes, please," he answered.

The same aide who'd shown him to this room stood in the door and said, "General Sokolov is ready to receive you."

"I'm coming." Werner straightened his dark suit and followed the soldier into the hallway, where the rest of the delegation was already gathered. Together they boarded the cars again, which took them to the former Wehrmacht engineer school in the suburb of Karlshorst that was now the Soviet Military Administration Headquarter (SMAD).

The impressive compound had weathered the war surprisingly well, which was probably the reason why the newly appointed city commandant General Sokolov had chosen it as his official residence. The main building stood proud amidst a park-like garden with an old tree population vested in lush greens.

Representative pillars lined the entrance to a three-story mansion made of gray stone that was the administrative headquarters, while smaller buildings in the back of the area hosted the barracked soldiers.

Even the majestic-looking long and small windows with bright white window frames had all the panes intact. Involuntarily, Werner held his breath, impressed by the dignity and beauty of this building.

General Sokolov was a stocky man with pitch-black hair and small brown eyes, who didn't waste time with niceties. He wasn't exactly good-looking, though he had a commanding presence. Extremely confident and forceful like all the generals were, he too had clawed his way up ruthlessly to the top. Werner was almost blinded by the medals and ribbons that covered the front of the man's uniform.

"Come and have a look," Sokolov invited them into his office, where a huge Berlin map lay on the table. The city was neatly divided into four occupation zones. The Soviet sector in the east of Berlin was slightly smaller than the three Western sectors together.

Werner wisely kept to the background but observed the general closely. He categorized him as the typical career officer with no patience for anyone with a different opinion, military and civilians alike. In that sense he was like all the others in the Red Army, but what separated him from the rest was the raw determination in his eyes. This man hadn't come to Berlin to take prisoners. Still, he'd be easy enough to get along with — as long as things went according to his wishes — but no doubt he would chew out their asses should anything stray from the plan.

And there was no doubt that plans had been made already.

"In the past weeks we have taken control of the city," General Sokolov said.

"And you have done this well," Gentner answered.

Sokolov sent him a dark stare that clearly indicated he did not appreciate interruptions, not even when they were meant to bootlick.

Werner had difficulties containing the tiny smirk threatening to appear on the corner of his mouth. Apparently, Norbert hadn't studied his new superior well enough. He caught himself at the thought and felt a tinge of remorse. It wasn't the wisest course of action to feel superior to his boss. Norbert might not be the iconic superman everyone touted him as, but he still held Werner's political fate in his hands. His best move would be to fully and completely side with his boss and back him up at every occasion.

Sokolov continued his illustration, tracing the map with a sharp pointer. "The police headquarters, the newspaper, the city hall, the municipal authority called the Magistrat, and the university are all in our sector, as you can see. And this is no accident."

Werner nodded. A well-thought-out plan.

"Furthermore, we control the surroundings of Berlin including railway routes, streets and waterways. We also have the sole functioning power station in our sector. If the Americans arrive in Berlin..."

He said if, not when, Werner thought. Stalin had meticulously planned ahead for a time after Hitler's downfall. Being the first ones to reach Berlin had been the key piece for all the others to fall into place. Swiftly installing communists in every position of the future city administration – which was the task of Gentner's group – would ensure the Western imperialists wouldn't get a foothold in the German capital.

It was a brilliant maneuver and once again Werner had to admit that the Great Old Man Stalin truly was a genius. He was up to every trick and always one step ahead of the rest of the world. That was one reason why everyone loved, admired, but also feared him.

"…they are presented with a fait accompli and will soon realize the futility of wanting to govern a part of this city which is deep inside Soviet territory. Sooner, rather than later, they will gladly leave Berlin to us and go home." Sokolov finished his speech and looked around, apparently inviting questions.

"What if the Americans don't go home?" the designated Chief of Police, Paul Markgraf, asked. Markgraf, a German tank destroyer troops captain, had been captured at Stalingrad. During his captivity he'd met Norbert, who had sent him to a four-month anti-fascist training program in Krasnogorsk, where he joined the National Committee for a Free Germany. Markgraf had the reputation of being a ruthless man who didn't shy away from unconventional methods to get what he wanted.

Werner didn't trust the burly man with the brooding expression and the neatly side-parted black hair combed to perfection with brilliantine.

General Sokolov waved the question away like a nasty fly. "They will, because they are weak. They are war-tired and wish nothing more than to send their boys home and leave Europe for good. But we are here to stay. We will govern not only Berlin, but all of Germany, and soon communism will reign from the Pacific in the East to the Atlantic in the West."

Emboldened by Sokolov's gracious response to Markgraf's

question, Werner asked, "What about the British and the French? They won't leave Europe, because it's their home."

"The French?" Sokolov scoffed. "A bunch of measly cowards who were overrun by the Wehrmacht in a matter of weeks. They never fought against the occupation and, frankly, it's beyond me to understand how they convinced the Americans to consider them a victorious power. They have contributed nothing to winning this war. The French will acquiesce to our ruling in the same way they capitulated to the Germans in 1940."

Sokolov looked around the room, pleased with his assessment of Europe's political affairs. "As for the British, they have shown some valor, that is not to be denied. But without the help from their American friends, Hitler would have invaded their petty little island years ago. They are no threat to us. They are as eager to leave the continent and retreat to their island as the Americans are eager to retreat across the ocean. As long as we assure the British that we have no interest in crossing the channel, they won't oppose us."

"Bravo!" Gentner clapped his hands and one by one the other men followed suit. This time General Sokolov was very pleased by the flattery and jovially invited them for a drink.

CHAPTER 2

M arlene carefully hid her long brown hair beneath the old and dusty cap, before she put on her only coat and said, "I'm going to look for something to eat."

"Be careful. The Russians..." her mother said with a deep furrow between her brows.

"I know, but we can't stay inside forever, or we will starve." Marlene glanced at her father, who slumped on the bed in the corner. He should be the one to go out and take care of his family instead of feeling sorry about the awful fate that had befallen them.

A wave of loathing hit her, but the next moment it washed over and left only pity for the broken man. Life had been hard on him. As a high-ranking government official, he had always provided for his family the best he could. They even lived in modest luxury – compared to most Berliners – until their building had endured structural damage during an air raid, and they'd had to relocate into the basement, along with the other surviving tenants.

It was understandable that her father felt weak and defeated. Because that's what every German was – defeated.

Capitulation. Unconditional surrender. Of course, nobody called it that. Instead people used the euphemisms *chaos* or *collapse,* as if it were something unintentional like a building collapsing after a direct hit, and not the utter, complete, and humiliating surrender to every whim of the new powers that be.

Reaching for the door, Marlene sighed.

"It's a disgrace! My own daughter sneaking into the streets like an urchin. Under Hitler there was always discipline and order! Everything was so much better!" her father shouted from the back of the room.

A shudder racked her shoulders. She didn't want to think about his words. Things were the way they were. Nothing she could change about the situation. Her energy was best spent coping with the circumstances instead of whining about them. Or trying to analyze…

"Yes, Father," she said and slipped out of the basement, emerging into a sunny but chilly May morning. The sun blinded her, and she blinked a few times. Berlin had been so beautiful before the war. She'd been fourteen when Hitler invaded Poland, but like all girls her age she was much more interested in play, boys, and clothes than in politics.

At first it had been nothing more than a distant excitement filled with celebrations for every newly occupied territory, but then the war drew closer. One by one her brothers, cousins, friends and neighborhood boys were drafted and sent away. Many returned in coffins, or not at all.

She shook her head, forcing the grief away. Nothing she could change about the past. Right now, her priority was to find food for her family, or they'd soon join the casualties of this war. Squaring her shoulders, she crossed the street and quickly faded into the shadows of the bombed-out buildings, always keeping away from the main streets.

It was best not to be seen by the Russians. The indiscriminate looting, murdering and raping were constant threats to anyone and especially for a woman. After a seemingly endless walk she reached the bakery, bathed in cold sweat.

"*Guten Morgen,*" she wished the baker's wife a good morning. "What do you have today?"

"No flour. No bread." The big woman scoffed. "*Ivans* came and took everything. Without paying, of course."

"I'm sorry, they're so awful," Marlene empathized with her.

The baker's wife squinted her eyes and looked unabashedly at Marlene's overcoat. "A nice coat you have. My mother is always freezing."

Marlene hated the ways things had become, but ration cards had lost their value long ago and it was only thanks to bartering that they'd been able to subsist for the past weeks. "And my mother is always hungry."

The woman nodded her understanding. "The *Ivans* might have overlooked a loaf. It's a bit hard, but still good."

"I'll take it." Marlene took off her coat and handed it to the baker's wife in exchange for a loaf of bread that was hard as stone. They'd have to soak it in soup to eat it, but it was precious food.

She put the bread into her bag and was leaving the bakery when her glance fell on a platinum-blonde woman walking down the street as if she owned it. Marlene sucked in a breath, aghast over how anyone could be so brazen. She fully expected a Russian to jump at the woman and shout the most feared words in Berlin at her.

Komm Frau! Come with me, woman! Just the thought sent violent shudders down her spine. The next moment the woman looked in Marlene's direction and Marlene stopped breathing altogether.

"Bruni? Is this really you?" she uttered, stunned.

"Marlene, what a surprise to see you here. How have you been?" Brunhilde von Sinnen, known as Bruni to her friends, looked incredibly radiant. She didn't have the cast-down, fearful appearance of most anyone else in this heap of rubble formerly known as Berlin. She took a few steps toward Marlene and hugged her tight. "Isn't it wonderful that I've found you? How are you doing?"

"Coping," Marlene said. But the next moment the happiness to see her friend again was replaced by unadulterated panic. A scowling Russian soldier walked toward them. "Bruni…we…an Ivan," Marlene's voice faltered.

But her friend barely moved her head and shrugged. "Oh, that's Gregori. He's my guard."

"Your guard?" Marlene's brain filled with impenetrable cotton wool and she didn't comprehend.

"Yes, silly." Bruni took Marlene by the elbow and said, "Let's go for a walk."

"A walk? Are you crazy?" Marlene still eyed the soldier called Gregori with suspicion, but he made no attempt to come closer than a few steps away.

"Not at all, I'm dying to catch up on news."

Marlene sighed and followed Bruni. Maybe there was strength in numbers and two women wouldn't be as much at risk as one.

"Isn't it a dream? The war's finally over and we're still alive," Bruni said with her incredibly beautiful voice.

"More like a nightmare," Marlene protested and told her about the godawful living conditions in the basement, how she had to take care of her parents, her constant fears and struggles.

Bruni came to a halt and looked at her. "When will you ever learn to look out for yourself instead of others, my dear? Look at you! Dressed in drab clothes, your beautiful hair hidden beneath that piece of filth...no wonder you're suffering. You need to adapt to the situation and find yourself a protector."

"A protector? Like your Gregori?"

Bruni giggled. "Of course not. Gregori is dispensable. He's a mere foot soldier, the kind women here are afraid of."

"Why not you?"

"Are you really that thick, sweetie? Once it was clear who the new bosses were, I put on make-up and my best dress and introduced myself to Captain Feodor Orlovski, commander of the technical corps in Berlin. There's only one man in Berlin more powerful than him, and that's General Sokolov himself."

"You threw yourself at a Russian?" Marlene spit out the words. How could Bruni sink so low?

"It doesn't matter with whom we associate, what matters are the reasons why we do it. These aren't normal circumstances. And I very much prefer to share the bed willingly with one man than unwillingly with many. To make sure nothing will happen to me Feodor has ordered his men to follow me at all times.

"Oh, Bruni. I'm so sorry...this is so awful." Marlene loved her friend dearly, despite her many faults.

"It's really not awful...Feodor is quite an accomplished lover." Bruni made a dreamy face. "He has the stamina of a trained soldier and the expertise of –"

"Stop. Please, no details." The rising embarrassment burned Marlene's face. She wasn't like Bruni, had only once given herself to her boyfriend on the day before he'd been sent to the front.

Bruni giggled. "In case you ever need womanly advice, I'd be more than happy to elaborate."

Her face burning, Marlene continued to walk down the street, almost forgetting the realities of Berlin while mulling over Bruni's trade with the devil. Was selling one's body to one man permissible if it prevented many others from stealing it?

They turned the corner into Marlene's street and Bruni gasped at the sight of the destroyed buildings. "How on earth can you live like this?"

"It's not that we have much choice," Marlene said. The next moment her stomach tied into a knot at the sight of two drunk Russian soldiers on the prowl. In her joy to see Bruni again, she'd neglected to scan the street and hide in time. Of course, they'd spotted the two young women and broad grins appeared on their dirty faces.

"Oh my God," Marlene whispered, bracing herself for the worst.

But it took only a few seconds until Gregori, who still followed them at a few steps distance, approached the two men and barked something in Russian at them. They looked dumbfounded and then turned on their heels.

"See how having a protector is beneficial?" Bruni said. "If you change your mind, I can certainly introduce you to a powerful and decent officer."

On trembling legs, Marlene said goodbye and retreated into her building.

CHAPTER 3

W erner was on his way to have a first look at the Berlin University. Both General Sokolov and Norbert Gentner had impressed upon him the importance of getting the education system up and running before the start of the new school year in September. And, just like that, he'd become the head of the department for culture and education.

An elite university akin to the one in Moscow – and naturally following the same political philosophies – was Stalin's explicit wish. And who would be brazen enough to deny the Great Old Man his dearest wish? Not Werner.

So, he set out to begin his Herculean task with the help of only two other men, both of them devoted communists who'd been liberated from a concentration camp mere weeks before.

Expecting a building similar to the SMAD headquarters, he gasped for air when he first set his sights on the university located on the prestigious boulevard *Unter den Linden* in the city center. His initial reaction was to refuse to set foot into the ruin that looked as if it would crumble at any moment.

"You sure this is where we are supposed to have the

lectures?" he asked Friedrich Effner, an emaciated gray-haired man in his early fifties who had survived the camps only thanks to his privileged position as a gifted accountant.

"Yes, I'm afraid so. It doesn't look all that bad, either," Effner answered.

"Well then, let's have a look inside." On their way in, they saw several Germans scurrying about searching for any suitable things to pillage. But the lecture halls and classrooms had already been cleared of all movable furniture. Only the bolted rows of benches with attached seats were left.

"Get everyone out of here, no more pilfering," Werner shouted at one of the soldiers accompanying his scouting group.

By a sheer miracle they found a back building with little structural damage and Werner chose the two best-preserved offices for himself and Effner.

"Herewith I make you the Dean of the new Berlin University," he said with a grin and motioned for Effner to take possession of his new office. "I'll get the technical company to commandeer furniture for us and we'll start tomorrow with the interviews."

"Yes, Comrade Böhm," Effner said.

Werner handed him a list of prospective professors the Soviet cultural ministry had given him. It was vital to start the anti-fascist education of Berliners only with the most reliable people. That ruled out most of the professors who'd still been working until recently.

After a lengthy discussion in the Gentner group it had been decided that the first faculty to open up, even before the official inauguration in January next year, would be medicine. Doctors were urgently needed, and Werner hoped that he'd find enough professors and students who weren't tainted by National Socialism.

"Are you considering screening the students for political reliability as well?" Effner asked.

In Moscow students were rarely chosen for their merits, but usually because of political rectitude. Of course, nobody ever admitted to this custom, but children of high-ranking party officials could get into any subject of studies, independent of their grades or personal achievements.

But this was Berlin. And Stalin had tasked them to build a demilitarized, democratic, anti-fascist society.

Werner had often thought about how to best complete the civilian-democratic revolution that had started in 1848. A land reform to abolish the remnants of feudalism was one thing, but erecting a democratic state with rights and freedom for the people, was a much more important, yet tricky, step.

He had seen the mistakes the Soviets had made during their implementation of communism, and in this instance he shared Anton Ackermann's opinion that in Germany, socialism could be reached without the prior dictatorship of the proletariat. Like the founder of the National Committee for a Free Germany, Werner believed in a "unique German way" to socialism and strongly objected to a Sovietization of the country.

But not politically screening the students could prove to be dangerous, too. What if one of them was swayed by imperialistic ideas and incited riots, geared toward destabilizing the young republic?

"Well, I think we need to screen them for fascist tendencies. We have to prevent dangerous Nazi elements from entering the university."

"That is an excellent idea, Comrade Böhm," Effner said. He was probably as afraid to fail at his new job as Werner was, since the party didn't forgive mistakes. "We could have the prospective students fill out an application form that asks not only for medical credentials, but also for former affiliations with Nazi organizations."

"We'll allow the first batch of students based on medical merit. Anyone who has studied before, or has served as a medic, will be given preference, except for those clearly involved with Nazi ideology. Draw up a form and show it to me tomorrow," Werner said, glad that he could delegate the tedious part of this process.

He left the office and made his way through the long hallways of the main building. He had office furniture to commandeer. On his way, he came upon a group of soldiers from the technical company carrying sinks to the exit.

"Hey, what are you doing here?" Werner asked their leader.

"Dismantling bathrooms for reparations," the engineer answered.

"No. You can't do this. This is the university building and we need the bathrooms when we're going to begin classes in the fall."

The engineer simply shrugged. "I have a task to do, now please get out of my way."

But Werner wasn't going to accept that his own people were endangering the re-opening of the university and stepped in front of the man, who was at least twice his size. In a gruff voice he clarified, "Comrade, I am Werner Böhm, head of the culture and education taskforce under Norbert Gentner."

The engineer perked up his ears at the mention of Gentner, but then shrugged again. "I have my orders. If you don't like them, get General Sokolov to issue new ones. And now will you please step out of my way, because I have work to do."

Werner looked at the sturdy, muscled man and decided he didn't want to start a brawl with him. Instead he rushed to the nearest military administration office and demanded to use the phone. Frenetically dialing Norbert's office number, he prayed that his boss was in.

"Gentner."

Thank God. "Norbert, this is Werner. I just left the university building and there's a group of Russian engineers dismantling the building."

"What do you mean by dismantling?" Norbert asked.

"They are removing the washbasins and even the toilet bowls and taking them away. Supposedly because this is part of the agreed-upon reparations to the Soviet Union." Werner almost laughed at the hilarity of the situation. Dismantling toilet bowls and shipping them to Moscow.

"Did you talk to their commanding officer?" Norbert didn't seem overly interested in the topic.

"Yes. He says he's under orders from General Sokolov." Werner saw another group of soldiers leaving the university building and throwing the porcelain pieces on top of a waiting truck. Judging by the noise, not many of the toilet bowls and washbasins would even make it out of Berlin in one piece. His desperation grew. If only the party allowed people to think for themselves.

Even though he knew this was just temporary, until the proletariat had been educated enough to understand complex connections, his anger rose. And, boy, did he wish for this temporary period to end right now.

"If it's signed by Sokolov, there's nothing we can do," Norbert said.

"You mean, I have to let them take away everything we need for the proper functioning of the university?" Werner was quickly reaching the end of his patience. Didn't Norbert understand how stupid this entire action was?

"I wouldn't go so far as to say you cannot ensure a proper

functioning just because these engineers are taking a few things for reparations."

"So, you think we don't need toilets for the professors and students?" Werner ran a hand through his short blond hair.

"Comrade, you're deliberately misinterpreting my words. The engineer has been ordered by Sokolov, so there's nothing we can do about it. If I were you, I'd concentrate on what is expected of me, instead of worrying about bathroom equipment."

Werner grimaced with disbelief and anger, glad that Norbert couldn't see him. He forced himself to even out his voice and then said, "I will do as you suggested. Thank you for your advice, Comrade."

He had just hung up, still furious about Norbert's unwillingness to help him, when another thought occurred. Despite knowing better, he simply couldn't let those brutes demolish what was left of the university without a fight. Even the most blockheaded Soviet official had to understand that it didn't make sense to dismantle the building just to install the stolen equipment again a few weeks later.

Maybe Captain Orlovski, the commander of the technical company, would appreciate if he saved him needless double work. He picked up the phone again and dialed Orlovski's number. After a short discussion Orlovski agreed to pause the dismantling until the two of them could meet in the afternoon.

Werner rushed to SMAD headquarters and at two o'clock sharp, he knocked at Orlovski's office door.

"Ah...you're Böhm. Your reputation precedes you, and I was wondering when I'd get to meet Gentner's protege, but never thought it would be so soon," Orlovski said instead of a greeting.

"Captain Orlovski, it's my pleasure. Please, excuse me for bothering you with this issue." Werner had heard that Orlovski was an engineer through and through, an intelligent man, always inclined to follow logic and reason. If he found the right words, the man might as well be on his side.

"Yes, yes, to the point. Why are you obstructing my men from taking the reparations that rightfully belong to the Soviet people?"

"Comrade, I may be a German by birth, but I'm a Russian by heart and thus I'm the first one to support the need of reparations for our beloved Soviet Union. The Nazi fascists have caused so much destruction to our country and it is only just that the Germans have to pay for what they did. But I am not sure whether the dismantling of lavatories and toilet bowls is actually helping rebuild Russia."

"That is the task of brighter minds than mine to decide. General Sokolov has ordered this task, so who am I to argue?" Captain Orlovski kept a straight face, but Werner believed he saw a flash of frustration in his eyes. So, the rumors were true and Orlovski had an independent mind.

But...he wouldn't get anywhere challenging authorities. The captain might be open to logic, but he was still an obedient soldier. Werner racked his brain for a different angle to the problem and said, "I am in complete agreement with you, Comrade. I must have expressed my opinion badly. Reparations must be paid. And I understand the need for swiftness, as we want to have the task accomplished before the Americans set foot into Berlin.

"But I wonder whether you couldn't fill your quota of bathroom equipment in other buildings, and especially in the boroughs assigned to the Western Allies, while sparing the university?" Werner hoped that Orlovski would follow the breadcrumbs and agree that it was more urgent to strip down the Western sectors, before the Americans made it to Berlin. It they were persistent enough to actually arrive here, that is.

"Comrade Böhm, why should I do this? The university has a total of 87 undestroyed lavatories and 64 toilets in good condition. That's close to five percent of my quota. And you will certainly agree with me that dismantling that amount of equipment from a single building is much more efficient than ravaging one hundred different buildings for one lavatory each."

Werner nodded. He understood the numbers. And now he knew Orlovski's concern. "I completely agree with you. The numbers would make sense to anyone reasonable. But, on the other hand, it might be beneficial for you to spare the university." Orlovski scowled and Werner hurried to add, "You see, I also have orders from Sokolov. Stalin himself wants to have an elite university that will stand up to any scrutiny from the imperialist West. The new Berlin University is destined to be an educational institution resembling the great University of Moscow, and will soon become the place where every German student wants to enroll."

Cold sweat ran down Werner's back. He wasn't lying. Norbert had boasted that Stalin himself had said such things. But his next words would be a slight stretch, and he would need to formulate them carefully to not get himself into hot water. "My only concerns are your time restraints."

Orlovski's eyebrows twitched up into an expectant smirk. "I'm sure they are."

"If you dismantle the bathrooms now, I will then have to make a request for new bathroom equipment a week from now. And then your men, who have worked so hard to strip the building, will have to return and install the same equipment they took out. This will cause your unit to waste precious time..." Werner stopped talking and let the captain draw his own conclusions about what course of action would be more beneficial for him. If Orlovski lived up to his reputation as an efficient engineer, he would despise the senseless double work.

A long pause ensued, during which Orlovski rubbed his chin. When he raised his voice again, he said, "I appreciate your concern for my unit. We are spread thin as it is, with the situation in Berlin and the urgency to present the Americans with a fait accompli. Therefore, I will grant your wish to spare the university, in the hopes this may benefit you and the cause of re-educating the German people in an anti-fascist way."

Werner understood what was expected of him. "Thank you for your consideration, Comrade. I, and the entire education department, will be deeply in your debt."

"Anything else you needed to discuss?" Orlovski asked.

"No, thank you. I am very grateful to you." Werner knew that at some time Orlovski would collect the favor he owned him, but it had been worth it. After all, he had to officially inaugurate the new Berlin University in little more than half a year. How, he had no idea.

CHAPTER 4

Marlene's mother boiled water on a portable kerosene stove, adding a few crumpled potatoes. Together with some hard bread, this would be their family's dinner.

As usual, father slumped on his cot, murmuring curses at the Russians and at the German traitors who had signed the capitulation. Marlene glanced at his face, contorted with hate and grief. *Poor man, he's lost so much.*

She feared for her father's mind but had no idea how to help him. Even her mother's determination seemed to deteriorate by the day. Marlene believed it was due to the fact that her parents never ventured outside. Who could stay in their right minds in this hellish, moldy, and dark basement? But as much as she begged them to go out into the streets, they always refused. *Too dangerous.*

But up there it wasn't much more dangerous than down here. If the Ivans wanted something, they simply knocked on the door. Her musings were interrupted by such a knock. The tension in the room flared like a sudden fire and three pairs of eyes were glued to the door. Marlene's breathing stopped.

This was her worst nightmare. It had happened before and everyone in the room refused to remember. With bated breath she waited, hoping the knocker would go away. After a while another, very faint knock.

Marlene got up, but her mother whispered, "Don't. The soldiers."

"Mother, please. The soldiers would knock more forcefully. Someone might need our help."

"You can't know this," her mother protested.

From outside the door sounded a shuffle and a desperate high-pitched groan. "It's a woman, for sure," Marlene said. "We have to open the door." She glanced at her father, but since he didn't even look in her direction, she forewent his approval and walked over to the door to open it.

"Oh my God! Whatever happened to you?" Marlene exclaimed at the same moment as the young woman standing outside staggered into her arms. Her formerly beautiful black waist-long hair looked like a matted bird's nest and her brown eyes were filled with horror. A gray-green dress, which must have been fashionable in a former life, hung in rags from her body, with dirt and dried blood smeared all over her.

"Marlene…" the young woman hissed.

Marlene recognized the voice, but it took her a while to match the face of this wretch to her childhood friend. "Zara…? Is this really you?"

Zara nodded. Feeling that her friend's legs were about to give out, Marlene grabbed her tight around the waist and dragged her into the basement room. Meanwhile Marlene's mother eyed the visitor.

"What are you thinking, to bring her inside? Who is this filthy person?" Mother scolded her.

"Mother, please, this is Zara Ulbert. Don't you remember

her?" Marlene responded, ignoring her mother's shocked face and leading Zara across the room to settle her on her own cot.

"You're not serious about letting her stay here? Look at her. I'm sure she's full of lice and God only knows what else."

Marlene looked at her mother with a stunned expression. "Can't you see that she's hurt and needs our help?"

"I can see that alright. But we can't help her, she needs to go to the hospital," Mother insisted.

"Oh...since you never venture outside, it must have passed by you, that there aren't any working hospitals right now. At least not for mere mortals like us." Marlene knew this was not an appropriate way to talk to her mother, but she couldn't help herself.

"One more reason to not let her inside. What if she's contagious? Has typhus? She's a threat to our safety." Mother pursed her lips, sending a helpless glance in the direction of her husband, who seemed too consumed with an old newspaper to even notice. He'd long stopped being the patriarch of the family.

"Mother, Zara used to be my best friend at school. How can you expect me to send her away when she is in need? Let me at least tend to her wounds," Marlene begged.

Zara, who hadn't uttered a word until now, made to get up. She stood on swaying feet and said, "I'm sorry. I shouldn't have come here."

"Yes, you should not have." Marlene's father suddenly joined the conversation. "Your father is a war criminal. Your very existence in our house is compromising us. Best if you leave right now."

Marlene looked back and forth between her parents and Zara. When had they turned into stonehearted monsters? Here was a badly injured woman, needing their help, and her mother was worried about lice, while her father feared being connected to a Nazi.

Zara had been Marlene's best friend, until Karl Ulbert had been transferred to occupied Poland four years ago. Back then her family hadn't known that Ulbert was one of the master-minds of the so-called death camps erected all over Poland and later became the commandant of the extermination camp in Mauthausen.

In post-war Germany he was one of the most-wanted war criminals. But her father's military career wasn't Zara's fault. Like Marlene herself, she was born in 1925, much too young to have played an active role in the Nazi hierarchy. Marlene shook her head in disbelief.

Zara apparently misunderstood the gesture and her shoulders slumped as she shuffled to the door.

A sudden iciness in her limbs impeded Marlene from moving and she watched her miserable friend reaching for the door. Then, a sudden burst of anger attacked her and she cried out, "No. Don't leave." She raised her chin and looked at her parents. "We can't let her go. She'll die without our help."

It wasn't clear who was more shocked by Marlene's open revolt against her father's wishes: her parents, or she. Trembling with fear and rage, she wiped all thoughts of future consequences aside, and reached for Zara. "Please lie down on my cot. I will get a doctor."

"Thank you," Zara whispered.

"Don't worry. I'll take care of you." Marlene fetched a glass of water for her friend and gave her a bowl of soup, ignoring the glowering stares from her mother. Then she covered Zara with a blanket and ventured outside to find the family doctor, Doctor Ebert.

He had known her since she was a baby girl and she was sure he would help. Outside, early summer heat engulfed her, but didn't stop her shivering. In front of her mother, she'd put on a brave face, but truth be told, she was scared to death every time she surfaced from the basement. She never wanted to relive the experience she'd had with one of the Red Army soldiers, shortly after the Russians occupied Berlin.

Dr. Ebert lived only a few blocks away, but it took her the better part of an hour to get there, because twice she needed to circumvent heaps of rubble she couldn't cross. With a thumping heart she knocked at his door.

His elderly mother opened, giving her a toothless smile, "If that isn't Marlene Kupfer. How have you been, my dear? Isn't it such a shame what is happening with our Berlin? But maybe we deserved it."

"Yes, Frau Ebert. Is Dr. Ebert here? A friend of mine is badly injured."

"Oh dear, he's not home. He's in the hospital. Would you like to wait?"

Marlene was surprised. "He works in a hospital now?"

"Oh no, not a real one like before the collapse. It's just an empty place where he takes the seriously ill. If you want you can find him there; it's two blocks down the street."

Marlene found the address easily. As Frau Ebert had mentioned, it was just a dilapidated building that miraculously had running water. She found the doctor up to his elbows inside the gut of a patient.

Her stomach recoiled at the repulsive sight, but the moment Dr. Ebert became aware of her presence, he barked an order without as much as a glance in her direction. "Hand me the needle over there, will you?"

She swallowed the vomit rising in her throat and did as she was told. Torn between disgust and curiosity, she opted to look the other way while the doctor stitched up the person lying on the cot.

"Knife wound," he explained and finally looked at Marlene. "Now. The bandage please." His hand pointed to a table filled with smudged bandages that definitely had been used before.

She picked one up and handed it to the doctor, who wrapped it around the waist of the groaning woman.

"Shush, shush. You'll be fine," he murmured in his deep soothing voice. Then he walked over to the sink to wash his hands and said to Marlene, "As cruel as it sounds, but these women would be better off not resisting the Russians forcing themselves on them."

Marlene swallowed. She didn't want to be reminded. Then she remembered the reason for her visit. "Dr. Ebert, can you come to my place, please? A friend has been severely injured, and I am afraid she won't make it without a doctor."

His shoulders slumped, and she noticed the utter exhaustion in his eyes. But it took only a few seconds for him to recover and nod his agreement. "Let me grab my bag." He packed some things into his huge doctor's bag and, before leaving the hospital, he pulled on a dirty white coat with a red cross on the back.

"That has proven quite useful," he explained, giving her a second one. "Even the Russians respect us medics, because they might need us one day."

Together they hurried to Marlene's apartment building and by a sheer miracle they weren't stopped or harassed on the way. Fifteen minutes later they stood in front of the basement door and she knocked three times. "Mother, Father, it's me, Marlene. I am with Dr. Ebert."

She heard a shuffling from the other side of the door and moments later her mother opened to let them inside. When she saw the doctor, she smiled. "Dr. Ebert, how nice of you to visit with us."

The doctor glanced slightly confused between her mother and Marlene. "I thought this wasn't a social call?"

"It's not. My friend Zara Ulbert needs your attention," Marlene hurried to say. Then she motioned for the doctor to follow her across the room to where Zara was lying motionless on the cot, with a pained grimace on her face.

"Zara Ulbert... Wasn't her father the commandant of Mauthausen?" Dr. Ebert asked.

"Yes, that's him," Marlene said, fear chilling her bones. Would the doctor refuse to treat Zara because of her father's crimes?

"I've heard half the Red Army is after him," he said, while kneeling down beside Zara.

"We didn't invite her in, she literally fell through our door," Mother said, following the doctor into the corner of the room. "And she cannot stay here. We were hoping you could take her with you."

Dr. Ebert ignored her and took a closer look at Zara. "Pretty badly roughed up," he murmured and opened his bag to examine the young woman. He demanded water and cleaned and stitched her wounds, the expression on his face growing more sorrowful with every passing minute.

When he was finished, he turned around and said, "Zara has a high fever and I'm afraid some of the wounds have been infected. This girl has been through a lot and needs constant care." He looked pointedly at Marlene's mother. "Frau Kupfer, while I agree with you that she would be better off in a hospital, there's no way to transport her, even if we found a hospital willing to take her in. As far as I know the only one currently operating is the Charité, and the Russian soldiers going in and out would have a feast with this young lady."

"But we can't keep her here," her mother protested. "We barely have enough space for ourselves, let alone food."

CHAPTER 5

Colonel Dean Harris was getting annoyed. His orders were to take an American reconnaissance unit into Berlin to take hold of their assigned boroughs. The convoy with over one hundred vehicles had reached the demarcation line at the Elbe bridge in Dessau hours earlier.

His superiors had warned him the Russians might be difficult and had urged him to stay composed, no matter what. But so far, the exact opposite had happened. The Russian Colonel Gorelik had behaved as if long lost friends had finally been reunited, and put up a welcome party that would put a royal wedding to shame.

Just a few minutes earlier, a Soviet sergeant had settled in front of a piano to play horrible tune after horrible tune. Dean was anxious to continue his journey, because from the demarcation line it was still over one hundred miles drive to Berlin.

For whatever strange reasons the Russians were playing for time, not wanting him to continue on his journey. But he didn't have the slightest inclination to stay in Dessau for one minute longer. His orders were to lead a reconnaissance unit to Berlin and he would do so, come hell or high water.

Dean got up and walked over to his Russian counterpart Colonel Gorelik. "Colonel, I must insist that we leave now."

Gorelik smiled at him. "Music nice, yes?"

Dean suspected that Gorelik spoke English well enough, and only pretended not to understand. He groaned inwardly and wished for his translator to be here, but the Russians wisely had invited only a few officers to the welcome party, leaving the rest of his roughly five hundred men to wait in the vehicles. His anger was bottling up inside and would soon explode, if nothing moved forward.

"Translator!" he demanded more harshly than he'd meant to.

Gorelik motioned for a sergeant to get the Russian translator, who'd conveniently disappeared half an hour ago. It took three more awful songs from the piano player until the man finally showed up.

Dean explained to him with the little patience he had left that he wanted to leave for Berlin this very instant.

"Certainly, Colonel Harris. We understand your eagerness to arrive at the capital and you're free to leave any time you wish."

"Great, thanks," Dean said, sighing with relief.

"But, one last question I must ask: How many officers, men and vehicles do you have with you?"

It was a strange question to ask, but by now Dean had seen too many Russian follies to think anything of it. They probably had counted the members of his convoy several times by now, so he saw no reason to be evasive. "Roughly five hundred men and one hundred twenty vehicles."

As soon as Dean's words had been translated, Colonel Gorelik shook his head with a sad face and said something in

Russian. The translator repeated his words in English, "The colonel is disconsolate, but the agreement allows only 37 officers, 50 vehicles and 175 ordinary men."

What the hell? Dean wanted to shake some sense into the blockheaded bureaucrats in front of him and asked with barely concealed aggression, "What agreement?"

The Russians seemed to enjoy the altercation and the translator coldly answered, "The Berlin agreement."

Dean didn't blink an eye, even though he had never heard of such an agreement before and was pretty sure it didn't exist. Although one could never be too confident that some off-handed diplomatic remarks hadn't been taken literally, and this was an honest misunderstanding. The urge to strangle both his superiors and the Russians for getting him into such a delicate position made the vein in his temple pulsate.

"I'm afraid I don't know of any such agreement," he hedged.

"Well, I do," Gorelik answered.

Dean thought for a moment about how best to tackle this issue. He couldn't well send home two-thirds of his convoy on the grounds of a mysterious treaty he'd never heard about. Seeing the lazy smile on Gorelik's face, he addressed the translator, "May I please see a copy of this Berlin agreement?"

The colonel hesitated for a moment and then said, "We only have a copy in Russian."

"That will do. I have people who can speak and read your language," Dean answered, wishing for his trusted translator Bob to be at his side right now. How much easier the entire conversation would be.

The Russian's face fell for a short moment, before he had his expression under control again. "Under these circumstances, I will have to check with headquarters."

"Well, then check with your headquarters," Dean hissed. Of course, the puppet had to check with headquarters. Did those damn Russians ever do something without checking with someone else first?

He balled his hand into a fist, wishing he'd never agreed to take on this mission. As far as he was concerned this was rapidly turning into a nightmare.

"As you wish, Colonel," Gorelik said. "I will immediately send a car to the village."

"The village?"

The Russian shrugged. "There's the nearest telephone line to Berlin."

What the fuck? Dean managed to swallow down the expletive, because it wouldn't help to contain the growing tension. He was sure that this was nothing but another ploy. The Russians had been in Dessau for almost two months and hadn't been able to establish telephone lines with their headquarters in Berlin? Impossible.

But General Clay personally had impressed on Dean not to cause any problems with the Russians and keep the mission peaceful – under any circumstances. So, he ground his teeth and waited. For two hours. Precious hours he could have been tackling the *Autobahn* to Berlin.

At least the Russians provided his delegation generously with champagne, beer, and white wine. What they didn't offer was the otherwise ubiquitous vodka. Dean wasn't sure whether this was meant as an affront or not. And he didn't really care. All he wanted was to leave this damned place and get on the road again.

When nobody returned with news from the Soviet headquarters, he finally exploded. "Look, I have orders to go to Berlin. These orders are clear and cover all my men and all my vehicles. What they don't say is, 'if the Russians are willing to let you pass.' Do you understand?"

"I'm afraid you will have to take up this point with my

superior, since I'm bound to follow the Berlin agreement," Gorelik said and kindly suggested, "Let me get him for you."

It took an agonizing forty-five minutes until a one-star general arrived and greeted Dean with the warmest welcome wishes. But despite supposedly being the man in charge, he repeated the same bullshit Colonel Gorelik had said and insisted that according to the elusive Berlin agreement they couldn't take more than the stipulated amount of men and vehicles through the Soviet-occupied zone.

Dean couldn't openly threaten the general, but he still made his opinion known and said, "I'm sure my superiors won't like this incident and it may cause repercussions. Our entry into Berlin was agreed to at the Yalta Conference."

The general wouldn't budge, be threatened, reasoned with or scared. He wouldn't be bluffed and couldn't even smile at a joke. Dean was at a dead end. He asked the general to let him talk in private with his deputy Major Jason Gardner, who was waiting in the car. Together they went over the options, which weren't many. Return to Halle or continue with only a third of the convoy.

"I say we return and ask for further orders," Gardner said.

Dean exploded. "No way I'm going to let those bastards win. If we give in now, who knows whether they'll ever let us drive up to Berlin."

"Dean, there are agreements in place..."

"...that they ignore at will and instead pull up some phony shit nobody has ever heard of. I tell ya it was a mistake letting the Russians get to Berlin first. Now we have to wrench every single inch of that damn city out of their damn hands."

"What do you suggest we do?" Gardner as always was the embodiment of calm reason.

Yes, what do to? He'd rather cut off his right arm than return to General Clay with his tail between his legs. "We split up. I take the allowed men to Berlin and you return with the rest to Halle, letting headquarters know what kind of block-headed bastards the Russians have turned out to be."

"You sure you should take on the Russians in your current mood?" Jason teased him, fully aware that Dean was about to explode at any moment.

Dean growled at his friend and then left the car to let the Russians know about his decision to submit to the mysterious Berlin agreement. If the general felt victorious, it didn't show on his face, and Dean was way beyond caring one way or the other. All he wanted was to leave this goddamn place and reach Berlin before nightfall.

Half an hour later after repacking everything, because the Russians insisted they weren't allowed to bring machine guns with them, Dean hopped into his jeep cussing a blue streak.

"At least we're moving and you'll see, it'll be a breeze to reach Berlin on the four-lane *Autobahn*," Bob, his driver and translator, said.

But after a few kilometers, the leading Soviet car pulled off the Autobahn and guided them along a cobblestoned secondary road.

"What the hell are they doing now?" Dean bumped his fist against the metal frame.

"No idea."

Dean waved down their escort and got out of the jeep, the vein in his neck pulsating dangerously. If those damn Russians didn't stop their antics right now, he'd crush their skulls. "Why aren't we going on the Autobahn as planned?"

The Russian shrugged, pretending not to understand.

"Autobahn?" Dean asked with growing frustration.

The Russian shrugged again and Dean's fingers twitched. He knew methods to make the bullheaded lout speak. But with superhuman effort he somehow managed not to strangle this so-called ally and instead motioned for Bob to join him.

"He says the Autobahn is under maintenance, therefore we have to take the secondary road," Bob translated, nervously eyeing Dean. He knew his boss's temper all too well and added, "Dean, you promised the general not to cause a diplomatic incident."

Dean gritted his teeth. The Russians were causing the incident, not him. Back in the jeep he growled, "We have every right to take our convoy into Berlin. So far, I've sucked it up and smiled, but these rotten bastards better not believe they can take me for a ride."

CHAPTER 6

"Zara, are you sure you can walk?" Marlene asked. They needed to go to the administration office and register Zara to receive a ration book for her. Although food was still almost nonexistent, without a ration book a person was doomed to starve.

"Yes," Zara pressed out between gritted teeth. Her breath was labored and she had shiny eyes, despite the fact that her fever had broken the night before.

"She can't return here," Marlene's mother said.

"But where shall she go? She has no place to live," Marlene objected.

"This is not our concern," her father joined the conversation. "She has been here for five days eating our food. Now she must leave. Her presence puts us in danger."

And what about her safety? Marlene wanted to shout. But it would be an unthinkable act of defiance to raise her voice against her father. Therefore she nodded and said, "Yes, Father."

For Zara's benefit she put on a brave face, but deep within she was worried to death. There was no way her friend would survive out on the street. Whilst walking the two blocks to the registry office, she racked her brain to find a place where Zara could stay. The only person who came to mind was Dr. Ebert. His makeshift hospital was always overcrowded, but he surely wouldn't send Zara away until Marlene had found her another place to live.

Dr. Ebert wasn't at the hospital, but a young man in his mid-twenties with curly brown hair and warm brown eyes greeted them: "How can I help you?"

"I am looking for Dr. Ebert," Marlene said. Zara slumped against the wall, barely able to hold herself upright. She was completely exhausted from walking just a few blocks.

The young man glanced at her and then back to Marlene. "I'm sorry, Fräulein, but he's not here. My name is Georg Tauber, by the way. I am helping Dr. Ebert with his patients."

"I am Marlene Kupfer and this is my friend Zara Ulbert." He visibly flinched at hearing the name and Marlene hesitated. He must have recognized Zara's last name and she felt a need to explain. "Dr. Ebert came to my house to treat my friend Zara several days back, but she can't stay with us and so I thought..." His kind eyes emboldened her to finish the sentence. "Can she stay here, please? Just for a few days until I have found her another place to live."

He nodded, giving her a smile that eased all her worries. "For the moment, yes. But Dr. Ebert needs to make the final decision, I am just helping out." He glanced in Zara's direction with barely concealed curiosity. Marlene basically *saw* the words forming at the tip of his tongue, but no sound came out. Instead he stretched his back and said, "Can you give me a hand and settle her on the cot over there, please?"

"Of course, Herr Tauber."

Together they led the stumbling Zara to a cot in the far corner of the room. The bedsheet was surprisingly clean, and Marlene wondered how they did the washing.

"Your friend is in pretty bad shape. What happened to her?" he asked.

"The usual." Marlene cast her eyes downward, attacked by disturbing memories. He seemed to understand, because he laid a gentle hand on Marlene's shoulder, as if to take away the burden weighing her down. She gave him a grateful smile. It had been a long time since she had received sympathy and compassion. Usually she was the one to console others.

In a move that was completely uncharacteristic for her, but too powerful to resist, she slung her arms around his back and pressed her face against his chest. No tears rolled down her face, but dry sobs shook her entire body, while he soothed her pain with long strokes of his hands down her back.

"Please, Fräulein, don't cry. It's over. You're safe here," he murmured again and again.

She knew he was lying, because nobody was safe in Berlin. The Russians could do whatever they wanted, even though the Americans had finally arrived a few days earlier, ending two months of agonizing Russian hegemony. Maybe now the constant raping, looting, robbing, and murdering would stop.

As her sobs eased, she became aware of her embarrassing behavior. Throwing herself at a virtual stranger, for the sole reason that he'd shown her some empathy that nowadays seemed to be in short supply. With a heated face, she stepped out of his arms, straightened her skirt and said, "Please forgive my inappropriate behavior, Herr Tauber."

His smile was sad and knowing. "No need to worry, Fräulein, we all need a shoulder to lean on once in a while. But please call me Georg."

"I am Marlene." She returned his smile, wondering what his

41

life's story was. His eyes didn't have the defeated look of desolation most everyone else wore these days. Instead they showed a suffering so overwhelming, it caused her physical pain. The shadows of his suffering went far beyond the daily struggle of survival experienced by every citizen in Berlin.

He wriggled under her scrutinizing stare and said, "Let's look after your sick friend, shall we?"

Zara was passed out cold on the cot, her skin heating up like an oven.

"She's not over the hump yet, the fever is back," Georg said. "I'm afraid she has developed an infection and will need penicillin."

"How do you know all of this?"

"Because I studied medicine. I was in my sixth semester, when I was drafted into the Wehrmacht."

"Oh," she said, wondering why he wasn't a prisoner of war.

Georg apparently could read her mind, or perhaps he simply had been asked that same question many times before, because he explained, "I served as a medic on the Eastern Front for about a year, before I returned to continue my studies. But it never came to that, since the Nazis didn't like me accusing them of the atrocities committed in Russia and sent me to the Mauthausen concentration camp instead."

"Oh." This certainly explained the pained expression in his eyes and his reaction to Zara's last name. What a grand man he was, helping the daughter of the very man at whose hands he'd suffered so much. She didn't know what to say, since she had never talked to a camp survivor before. One thousand questions burned on her lips. *Was it as bad as they say? What did they do to you? How did you survive?* Instead, she studied the tip of her shoes, feeling the shame trickling into every fiber of her body and soul. Could she have known? Should she have known? Could she have done something?

In hindsight, the signs were clear. But like everyone else she had closed her eyes to what was happening. Not even the excuse to have been so young when it started was valid. Despite her tender age, she could have known, could have opposed. Could have begged her parents to do something. But she didn't. Because she had lived comfortably in the modest luxury her father, a government official, had provided them.

A frightening thought grabbed her. Her father must have known, perhaps even assisted in the awful things. *No, no, no,* she violently brushed the awful suspicion away. *No!* Her father was a good man who worked for the labor bureau. He'd never mentioned anything about these crimes. Their home had always been an island of calm in the eye of the storm. She had not even noticed that a war was going on until her two brothers had been drafted in 1941.

Her brother Kurt had written glowing letters from Paris, making it sound like an endless party. A party she had been jealous not to be allowed to join. Only when the English and American bomber squads had begun discharging their deadly cargo over Berlin, night after night and day after day, had she finally understood what war really meant.

It meant death, destruction, grief, sorrow, hunger, pain, and cold.

"Hey, Marlene, are you all right?" Georg's voice tore her out of her thoughts.

"I'm fine. I'm just..." She sighed. She felt inadequate to express her sorrows, especially in front of a person who had lived through so much worse than she probably could ever imagine. "... I just have never met anyone who was in a concentration camp."

He gave her a lopsided smile. "It's nothing to aspire to."

"I'm so sorry," she said.

Before they could continue the conversation, Dr. Ebert

entered the room and said, "Marlene, what a surprise! How is your friend?"

"She was getting better, but the walk here has exhausted her and the fever returned," Marlene answered.

Dr. Ebert shook his head. "You shouldn't have come here. The walk was too strenuous for her weakened condition."

Georg joined the conversation. "I'm afraid she has an infection and will need penicillin."

"And where should I get this?" Dr. Ebert muttered beneath his breath. "It's not like I can just walk into a pharmacy and buy it."

Marlene gave a nervous giggle. The idea of doing such a mundane thing as walking into a pharmacy seemed utterly ridiculous, given that Berlin had been dubbed the world's biggest heap of rubble.

"The black market," Georg said.

"Too dangerous," Dr. Ebert refused. "I just came from there. The Russians are raiding the area in an attempt to cut down on contraband. We need to wait a few days until the whole commotion settles down."

"It might be too late by then."

Marlene's heart missed a beat as she heard his words. She couldn't just wait and let Zara die. Something must... *Bruni!* Her new lover, the Russian captain. Maybe he could help. She didn't tell the two men about her plans.

"I forgot I need to run some errands and will return in the afternoon," she said, turning on her heels to hurry off.

"Wait, I'll send Georg with you..." Dr. Ebert shouted after her.

The doctor's kindness warmed her heart. He was already the second person this day to show honest concern for her. Her parents had long given up caring for anyone or anything besides themselves. She scolded herself for the unworthy thought. Her father had provided many years for the family, he deserved a break. It wasn't his fault. The desolate situation had gotten to everyone, demoralizing even the bravest and strongest.

And her mother was forgivably stricken with grief, because she hadn't heard news from either one of her two sons. A flash of anger ripped through Marlene's body. Her mother would gladly exchange Marlene's life for the life of one of her sons, since she was just a girl. The flare of fury dissipated as quickly as it had appeared and she came up with excuses for her mother. *She doesn't mean it. She's overwhelmed, crazy with grief.* But a bitter taste remained. She hurried to Bruni's place hoping to find her friend at home.

Bruni opened the door dressed in a nightgown. "What are you doing here at this ungodly hour?"

Marlene frowned. It was nearing noon and any decent person would be awake. "I need your help."

"Come in. What's it this time?" Bruni had the tendency to sound rather obnoxious, but Marlene knew that deep inside her friend was a kindhearted person.

"It's about Zara, she needs penicillin."

"Zara? I thought she was in the occupied territories? Oh well, they're not occupied anymore. At least not by us." Bruni smirked.

"Zara showed up at my house about a week ago, badly beaten up and, you know…" Marlene shrugged. "Anyhow, she caught an infection and Dr. Ebert says if she doesn't get penicillin soon, she will die."

"You can't get penicillin anywhere in Berlin. It's not as if you could walk into a pharmacy and buy it."

Marlene laughed. "That's exactly what Dr. Ebert said. I

thought maybe… I mean your Russian captain, maybe he could get some."

"He's not a medic." Bruni raised her eyebrows, clearly indicating what she thought of Marlene's plea. Then she sighed. "Alright. I will ask him. But I can't promise anything."

"I love you. Thank you so much."

CHAPTER 7

Werner entered General Sokolov's spacious office with the dark wooden panels on the walls and the prestigious white ceiling crisscrossed by wooden bars painted in gold. It must be an important occasion, because all the Russian officers and German Muscovites were there.

"Comrades," General Sokolov raised his voice, returning everyone's attention to the meeting. "Reparations are too slow. The target is ten billion Reichsmark worth and the actual amount is far beneath what Moscow expects. You need to redouble your efforts and repatriate more valuables to the Soviet Union."

Uncomfortable mumbles spread through the room. There was a reason for the slowdown in sending reparations to Russia, but nobody dared to tell the general.

Finally, Captain Orlovski raised his voice, "Comrade General, we certainly agree with your assessment, but the Americans have tightened their stance and won't allow us to take anything out of their sector. They even have seized our trucks at the sector limits and forced us to unload captured reparations."

Sokolov's fist slammed onto the table and his irate voice cut through the ensuing silence. "That's illegal! An affront to our sovereignty! We have a right to these reparations. They were agreed to in the Potsdam Conference."

Again, nobody dared to say a word.

"This is an incredibly vicious move by these imperialists to hurt our people." General Sokolov raged on about the despicable Americans and how the peaceful world would be better off without their constant warmongering.

Werner had met several Americans over the course of the past weeks. Much to his surprise, all of them had been friendly laid-back fellows, open to reason. In this particular issue he even sided with their position. It was detrimental to Berlin's reconstruction to dismantle everything without thought or reason – as had almost happened at the university. Naturally, he never uttered a single sound about that.

He might not agree with everything the Soviet Command decided, but certainly they must know best, because they had the full picture. It wasn't his place as a lowly party official to question the decisions made higher up the hierarchy.

"When will the radio station be up and running, Comrade Gentner?" General Sokolov asked. It was another directive shoved down on them that had to be enforced within days, and Werner had been the unfortunate person chosen to scout for a place to host the editorial office.

"Comrade Böhm has identified a suitable location in our sector," Gentner answered, cleverly pushing the responsibility away from himself.

Cold sweat trickled down Werner's forehead. He'd wanted to search for another location, because he hadn't had the heart to evict the current tenants.

"Great. When did you move in?" Sokolov asked and Norbert Gentner peered expectantly at Werner, motioning for him to answer.

"Not yet, General…there is a problem." Werner could see the tic in Sokolov's eye, a sure sign that he was annoyed. "It's just…there's a hospital in the building and I thought…"

"A hospital?"

"An unauthorized place to treat Germans set up by a German doctor," Norbert offered.

Sokolov moved his hand as if shooing a fly. "Evict them. I expect the first issue of the *Tägliche Rundschau* to be published by the end of this week."

"Yes, General, of course." Werner acquiesced and took out a kerchief to wipe the sweat from his forehead. As much as he hated the idea of evicting bedridden patients for the benefit of an editorial office, there was no way to openly defy the general's orders.

He consoled himself with the notion that it didn't affect innocents. The Germans had started this war and deserved everything they were getting. Only after a thorough re-education, in which he would play an important part, could they earn the trust and benevolence of the Soviet people.

Thankfully General Sokolov moved on to the next matter on the agenda and seemed to have forgotten about Werner's shortcomings. But Norbert hadn't.

As was customary, after all the official agenda points had been worked on, the informal part of the gathering began, with vodka flowing generously to celebrate the victorious end of the war.

In twenty years of living in Moscow, Werner never understood what the Russians liked so much about this beverage, but he had learned to drink like a local. Still, he preferred wine or beer, but for obvious reasons would never say so. The party demanded absolute obedience and even something as innocuous as not liking vodka might be considered, if not betrayal, then at least a suspicious act of defiance.

"Great stuff, directly imported from Moscow," Captain Orlovski toasted with his full glass.

"Sure is," Werner replied politely, raised his own glass and swallowed it in one big gulp. The soft burn ran down his throat and caused a warm feeling in his stomach.

"More?" another officer asked with the bottle in hand.

"Yes," he said and downed the second glass as quickly as the first one. Thanks to years of training, he could easily drink half a bottle without feeling the effects.

Orlovski grinned with appreciation. "You might be a German, but you drink like a Russian."

"Thanks for the compliment, Comrade." Werner put the empty glass on the next available surface. "It comes in handy when mingling with the Western diplomats. Their tongues loosen at the latest after the second glass."

Both Russian officers guffawed. Orlovski held his glass with the pinky finger stretched out and added in a mock French accent, "Especially the French, who only drink their sophisticated wine." Roaring laughter followed, and Werner hurried to join his comrades in mocking not only the French but all the mollycoddled Westerners who didn't know how to drink hard liquor.

Getting them drunk was a preferred method to gather intelligence. Fill the foreigners up to the toby collar with vodka and listen to them spilling the beans. Approximately an hour later, Norbert approached him and led him into a quiet corner.

"What was all that about? You're shedding a bad light on me with your reluctance to follow orders," Gentner demanded to know.

"I'm sorry. It's just..." He probably shouldn't voice his

concerns, but the alcohol had loosened his tongue and decreased his mental alertness. "I'm worried about our image with the German populace. The horror inflicted by our troops does nothing to endear them to us. On the contrary, they are turning with open arms to the Americans, who are much softer in their treatment of civilians."

Many officers had hinted, in private conversations, at their dislike for the behavior of the troops and Werner believed Norbert would agree with his assessment.

But Norbert said coldly, "This is not a problem you should concern yourself with. Moscow knows what is opportune to do or not to do. If they think the violence should stop, then they will stop it." He looked at the younger man and added, "There aren't enough women in the Red Army and our poor boys have fought so hard, they deserve the distraction of a warm body."

"You know as well as I do that it's not the combat troops showing the worst behavior, but fresh troops coming in from Mongolia who have done nothing for the liberation of Berlin." The words stumbled out of Werner's mouth before he could prevent it.

Gentner glowered at him. "You are wrong. And I advise you not to question the supreme wisdom of our party. Instead of feeling pity for the civilians, invest your energy in getting that radio station up and running. Leave the rest to the bureaucrats in Moscow."

Werner swallowed down a sharp remark and said instead, "Yes, Comrade, first thing in the morning I'll evict the hospital patients to make room for the new editorial offices."

A stale taste remained. He loved Russia and communism, but Stalin's interpretation of Leninism-Marxism was one of terror, torture and murder. Lenin would turn in his grave if he knew of the crimes committed in his name. *No, that's not fair.*

We're still in the transition phase where some sacrifices must be made. Finding excuses for behavior the party wouldn't tolerate in any other country or person had become so deeply ingrained in Werner's personality that he didn't even notice it anymore.

About an hour later, Werner made to leave the party. He knew the Russians would soon get completely sloshed and if he stayed one minute longer he'd have no choice but do the same. Then he'd sleep in with the rest of them, unable to get up before noon. And he wouldn't be able to evict the hospital patients in time...

But just as he reached the exit door, the sentry asked him to follow him. Cold fear gripped his heart. Often people disappeared, never to be heard from again. Both his parents had suffered this fate after a social midnight call from the NKVD.

It was Werner's luck that he'd been away on a field trip with his Komsomol unit or he might have joined his parents on their trip to an unknown future. Rumor had it they'd been relocated to a beautiful rural village in Siberia. He'd clung to this story for as long as he could, but when he didn't receive as much as a single letter in years, he'd finally accepted that their true fate must have been a very different one.

The guard led him to Sokolov's private office and told him to sit down, before leaving the room. Werner was covered in cold sweat, his heart racing. He calculated his chances to make it out of the compound alive should he try for a run, and decided it was better to stay. The dreadful time of the purges was long over. He hadn't done anything wrong. Had nothing to fear.

He sat motionless in his chair, trying to exude an air of confidence. Still, the minutes ticked by excruciatingly slowly and he started to squirm in his seat. Would they punish him for his criticism? Send him back to Moscow? To Siberia? To a gulag?

Drops of sweat formed on his forehead and he longed to swipe them away with his kerchief, but that would acknowledge his nerves and be seen as a sign of guilt. An innocent person didn't have a reason to be nervous. Glancing at his wristwatch he noticed that one hour had passed, when finally the door opened and Sokolov himself stepped inside.

Werner swallowed hard. The situation was graver than he thought.

"Werner Böhm?" Sokolov asked as if he didn't know him.

"Yes, Comrade General, that's me."

"You have been a stellar member of your Komsomol and you have graduated with honors from Moscow University in philosophy, politics and foreign languages."

"Yes, General. It was an exceptional honor to study at such a great institution and I'm beyond grateful for the opportunity." Werner did what was expected of him, hoping for some lenience for his earlier out-of-line behavior.

"Well, it is a strange way to show your gratitude criticizing the very people who allowed you to study." The general squinted his eyes, but couldn't suppress the nervous tic.

Panic froze Werner's blood and he almost wished for lightning to strike him right there in the general's office. Somehow he managed to keep his voice bland. "I am very sorry, General, it was not my place to speak up. I got carried away by sympathy for the patients."

Sokolov didn't show any sign of emotion. "I am tired of your constant nagging. You seem to believe that you are smarter than the rest of us, but let me tell you: that's wrong. You are nothing. Worse than nothing, because your parents were traitors. They came to the Soviet Union pretending to be communists while in fact they acted as spies for the fascist imperialists."

Fear and anger snaked up Werner's spine. His parents weren't fascists and certainly not spies or traitors.

"It's only thanks to Stalin's kind indulgence that you were allowed to stay in Moscow, because he believed you to be a good student. Was Stalin wrong to put his trust in you?"

Werner blanched. There was only one way to answer this question. "Of course not, General, Stalin is never wrong. It is completely my own lack of farsightedness that led me to occupy my mind with questions that are far beyond the scope of my average brain."

"Well, I wouldn't say your brain is average. You are quite intelligent and it seems Comrade Gentner holds you in high esteem. And he is the only reason why I will let you go with a warning this time. But rest assured, this is the only warning you will ever receive. From now on you will not question your orders, the party line, or any single word coming down the chain of command. You will completely and fully embrace our activities in Berlin, whether they are directed at the German population or our so-called allies. If I ever hear another complaint or suggestion coming from you, this will be the last thing the world has heard from you. Are we clear?"

"Perfectly clear, General. And thank you for the opportunity to show my dedication to the communist cause." The self-humiliation and brown nosing came easily after decades of practice, although a slight queasiness in his stomach remained. The liberation of Berlin had proved a stark disappointment and sown a seed of discontent with the reigning doctrine.

For now, he'd cling to the hope that in due time, things would change and the Germans would embrace the advantages of the communist system. They would forget about the initial cruel treatment endured at the hands of the Red Army and would embrace their new friendship with Russia. After all, the Russians had come to Berlin with the best intentions. They were here to bring to Germany freedom, wealth, and democracy.

"Dismissed." General Sokolov turned around and left the room; Werner followed several seconds later. While walking the short distance to the car waiting for him in the parking lot, he vowed to suppress from now on any and all individual thoughts and work strictly according to his orders.

He'd start with ruthlessly evicting the hospital patients in the morning.

CHAPTER 8

F inally, Marlene had found a useful task. Her parents were constantly complaining about the hardships that had befallen them and, frankly, she'd scream if she must hear it one more time. How much more satisfying it was to spend her time tending to badly injured people and experiencing their gratitude.

Every morning she rushed to the hospital as soon as she woke. But that day she was in for a horrible surprise. A group of Russian soldiers had infiltrated the building, forcefully evicting the patients and confiscating every piece of furniture. She pressed her back against the wall, waiting for two soldiers to pass her, before she slipped inside looking for Dr. Ebert.

Her glance fell on a rather smart young man who barked orders in Russian at the soldiers. But he wasn't in uniform, which was peculiar. Instead he wore a dark blue business suit consisting of pants with a sharp crease and a well-fitting jacket.

The man noticed her and crossed the room to approach her, giving her ample time to study his gait and face. He seemed well-educated, poised and definitely in charge of whatever was happening here. His blond hair was cropped short and he had alert gray-green eyes. She judged him to be in his late twenties, but nowadays it was so difficult to tell. He could be much younger, because he didn't have the worn-out, battle-hardened expression most soldiers, even the youths, wore.

He didn't look Russian at all and she could have sworn he was German, which was all but impossible. A German barking orders at Russian soldiers?

"Fräulein, are you in charge of this place?" he asked in perfect accent-free German. But what surprised her most was his soft tone, unlike the usual bellowed commands the Russians issued.

"No, *mein Herr*, that would be Dr. Ebert. I'm just an auxiliary nurse."

He smiled and his formerly cold eyes exuded warmth, while he stretched out his hand. "I'm Werner Böhm, in charge of the culture and education taskforce of the Soviet High command."

"Marlene Kupfer," she said, unsure what to think about him. This Herr Böhm seemed nice enough, but apparently, he worked for the Russians.

"I'm pleased to meet you, Fräulein Kupfer, and while I certainly applaud the work you're doing here, unfortunately my orders require me to inform you that this is an unauthorized operation and you must vacate the building as of today." The green of his eyes faded into a cold gray and he looked honestly sorry.

Marlene couldn't help but blurt out, "Unauthorized? Are you kidding me?"

He raised an eyebrow before answering, "Fräulein Kupfer, I can assure you this is not a joke. Your little hospital is a sanitary danger to national health. My orders stipulate that this operation has to be shut down immediately."

"I can't believe you monsters remove bedridden patients under some phony rules!" Marlene was livid. She balled her hands into fists and would have strangled the man in front of her if it hadn't been for Dr. Ebert's intervention, who'd appeared like a ghost behind her.

"Herr Böhm, I beg you to pardon my nurse. She is still young and temperamental. I will see that your orders are fulfilled. But would you be so kind as to tell your soldiers to leave the handling of the patients to us?" Dr. Ebert didn't flinch. He was a man who had seen everything and there was nothing that could get him upset.

Marlene glared daggers at the poor doctor, but she reluctantly accepted that it was no use resisting the occupying authority. Things only got worse when people put up a fight. Most of the patients in this room could testify to this fact.

Even though Herr Böhm looked pleasant enough, he was as much a monster as the rest of the Russian devils. These so-called liberators behaved worse than the Nazis ever had.

"Thank you, Dr. Ebert. To reward your cooperation, I will give you until tomorrow morning to vacate the building," Böhm said, glancing expectantly in her direction.

Did he expect her to be grateful for his generosity? Not until hell froze over. Self-righteous bastard. But a nudge from Dr. Ebert made her put a good face on the matter. With her sweetest smile she said, "Thank you very much for this incredibly humane and considerate offer. It's an honor to attend to the orders bestowed upon us by the Almighty Soviet High Command."

Herr Böhm's face took on a pleased expression, but when he noticed the poisonous sarcasm in her voice, he suddenly looked as if he'd chewed on a lemon.

She rejoiced at the small victory. But not for long.

A lazy grin crossed his face. "If this is your wish, I'm sure one of my Mongol soldiers would be willing to bestow his attention upon you, Fräulein Kupfer."

An icy hand gripped her heart and Marlene wished to shrink and disappear into a bomb crater. He couldn't be serious about his threat, could he? Thankfully she didn't have to explore the seriousness of Böhm's words, because Georg entered the room.

"What's going on here?" Georg asked, concern written all over his face.

"The Soviets have come to evict us, because our hospital hasn't been properly authorized," Dr. Ebert explained.

Marlene noticed the deep crease forming on Georg's forehead, even though his voice was calm. "You're serious, aren't you?"

"I am very serious, as is this gentleman here." Dr. Ebert pointed at Böhm. "Herr Böhm is a member of the Soviet military government and chairman of the culture and education taskforce of the Gentner group."

Georg's head swiveled around with an expression of disbelief in his eyes. The two men were about the same age, but couldn't look more different. The Muscovite was blond, tall, and had an air of authority about him, while the German was shorter, thinner, with brown hair and friendly brown eyes.

During the past days Marlene had come to appreciate Georg's warmth and kindness. He had a God-given talent for handling the patients and never once raised his voice even during the most frustrating moments. She knew he would become a great doctor once he could take up his studies again.

Böhm seemed to feel the need to say something and raised his voice. "I am truly sorry for the inconvenience. I'm merely following my orders and I trust that you will have it vacated by tomorrow morning."

Marlene glared at him, but knew better than to engage him again. He was a monster. Like all the Russians.

"Why would the Soviet Command do such a thing?" Georg asked as soon as Böhm had left the building, the soldiers trailing behind. "They must not be aware of the dire situation."

Georg was a bright young man, but he was also very trusting, always believing in the good in people. There was just one problem — the Soviet governors weren't good people. As far as Marlene was concerned, the bastards were obsessed with power and had little concern for individual lives.

"What are we going to do now?" Marlene asked.

"I don't know." Dr. Ebert's shoulders slumped and he suddenly looked aged beyond his years. He had worked miracles, after Bruni's lover had organized the penicillin, and Zara was on the way to recovery. Marlene was forever indebted to him and she wished she could comfort him, tell him everything would be all right.

"I may have an idea," Georg said. "Let me check, I'll be back in an hour." Even before he finished speaking, he sprinted from the building, leaving Marlene and Dr. Ebert wondering what he was up to.

As promised, he returned about an hour later with a bright smile on his boyish face. "I found a room!" He blurted out. "It's in the American sector, and it's perfect. It has running water. And electricity. This is so much better than what we have here, and I already talked to the American administration and they are okay with us using the entrance hall for our field hospital."

"That's such fantastic news." Marlene hugged Georg and even Dr. Ebert mustered a smile.

"We should move right away. Better not run into those thugs again tomorrow," Marlene suggested.

"They aren't all bad. Berlin is a mess and they need to adapt first." Georg as always tried to see the positive in every person.

"Well, they could have adapted without forcing themselves on every woman in town and stealing every last valuable object," Marlene growled. As nice as Georg was, why on earth did he have to defend the Russian monsters?

"I agree, that wasn't appropriate, but this behavior has stopped. The Soviet Command probably had no idea their troops were going on a rampage like that."

Marlene glared at him, "Why do you still believe the Russians have a single good bone in their bodies? Evidence suggests otherwise."

"We have to give them a chance. They came here to implement an anti-fascist and democratic government. This cannot be done in a few weeks; therefore we need to be patient and in two or three years from now we can judge them on their merits."

As far as Marlene was concerned, she didn't want to wait three years. She had made her decision the moment the Americans arrived and miraculously had not behaved the same way as the Russian beasts. The Americans were another unwelcome occupying power and she wished them gone sooner rather than later, but in their presence, she at least didn't have to fear for her physical safety.

CHAPTER 9

Dean had learned to hate the meetings in the Allied Kommandatura with a passion. It was the governing body of Berlin, consisting of the commandants and their deputies of each of the four victorious powers.

He didn't doubt the good intentions of the statesmen who'd decided at the Yalta Conference to govern Berlin as a quadripartite city by unanimous vote. But the Soviets had turned the institution into a veritable battlefield with them on one side and reason on the other.

It wasn't any different on this day, when General Sokolov complained, "This behavior is an affront to our sovereignty and cannot go unpunished!"

Dean felt the pulse in his temple and whispered to his translator, "What's he want this time?"

"More reparations," Bob hissed.

"Oh no! Not the reparations again. Haven't they already stolen everything that's not nailed down?" Dean leaned back in his chair. Sokolov was on a roll and that meant more endless hours of abuse. Why, oh why, had Eisenhower refused to attack Berlin and given the Soviets first dibs?

As Dean had expected, Sokolov launched into a lengthy tirade about the great Soviet Union and their courageous war heroes who had borne the brunt of the Nazi attack and single-handedly won the war. He elaborated on how the Red Army had broken the backbone of the Wehrmacht in Stalingrad and thus deserved all the praise, while the Western Allies actually had done little to nothing except in the last throes of the war, which didn't do much more than shorten it by a few weeks at most.

Everybody in the room, including Sokolov himself, knew this wasn't true. It was the American Lend-Lease Act in 1941, under which thousands of locomotives, rail cars, aircraft, trucks, machine guns, ammunition, medicine and whatnot, were given to the Soviets, that had made the victory at Stalingrad possible.

"It's intolerable that our military personnel are held back at the sector border and our trucks are searched before being allowed to cross." Sokolov stared directly at Dean, and waved a document as he continued, "Here it clearly states that military personnel of the victorious powers are free to move around *all* of Berlin."

Dean sighed. He knew he'd get a mouthful from General Clay as soon as the Soviets took this up to the superordinate Allied Control Council, which effectively had the same function for all of Germany as the Kommandatura had for Berlin.

"General, please, let's stick to the facts. You had two months to pilfer every single object of value from Berlin." Dean noticed with delight how Sokolov's face reddened. "And you may continue to do so in your own sector, but I warned you several weeks back that your soldiers are not welcome to come to our boroughs and steal what belongs to us."

"In the Yalta Conference we were awarded ten billion Reichsmark!" Sokolov shouted.

I'm sure you have extracted more than that already. Lying thieves that you are. Dean was wise enough not to voice his thoughts, because he didn't want to stir up unnecessary trouble. His own government was filled with appeasers, bowing to every Soviet whim, somehow hoping they would change and become model world citizens if the West acquiesced to enough of their demands.

Hadn't those appeasers learned their lesson with Hitler? The Russians were the world's biggest liars, thiefs, and hoodlums, intent on skinning their trade partners alive. They couldn't be trusted, because they promised anything, signed anything, provided it was beneficial to them, and then would scrap the pledge the moment it didn't suit them anymore.

"Nobody said you'd get them all at once and certainly not by stealing from our sector what we need to rebuild the city. I will hold up your trucks at the sector border until you stop stealing from us," Dean said and noticed with joy the helpless expression in Sokolov's face.

The French and British commandants both kept quiet, which Dean had come to expect. The Frenchman rarely said a word and if he did it was to diplomatically calm the waves, while the Englishman might rant and throw hissy fits, but never come into open confrontation with Sokolov.

Apparently, the only person standing in the way of Russian dominion over Berlin was Dean. The burden weighed heavily on his shoulders and he lay awake at night, trying to conjure up ways to keep the Soviets from stealing the city from under his ass. He'd even resorted to sleeping with his pistol under the pillow, thanks to anonymous death threats and telephone terror that he attributed to the Russians.

But if Sokolov believed he could wear him down, he'd come

up against the wrong opponent. Dean wasn't called block-headed for no reason, and the more stumbling blocks Sokolov threw between his legs, the more firmly he set his ambitions on resisting him.

~

Dean asked his driver to take him to the Café de Paris. The nightclub was in the French sector and had the reputation of having the best food, the most talented singers, the most beautiful waitresses, and plenty of pretty women willing to keep an Allied officer company. Just what he needed to wind down after ten grueling hours of not reaching a single common point at the Kommandatura.

The Café de Paris did not disappoint, and he had just settled at the table with a group of French officers he knew when a new singer stepped onto the stage. She was announced as Fräulein von Sinnen and looked absolutely stunning with her shiny platinum-blonde hair carefully combed into soft waves. Her beautiful face with blue eyes was styled to perfection with whatever tricks women used to make their eyes appear big and bright. She wore a full-length glittery silver dress with thousands of sequins sewn onto it that hugged her female figure like a glove – both the dress and the soft curves were a rare remnant of Berlin's grandeur before the capitulation.

He wondered what Fräulein von Sinnen's backstory was and how she'd managed to elevate herself above millions of miserable, starving women in the capital. There simply wasn't enough food in the city to properly feed the population, not even on the black market.

Officially, Dean frowned upon the black market, but he rarely ever took any action against it, especially not since his archenemy Sokolov had chosen to aggravate the food situation further by using the produce from the neighboring states Brandenburg and Mecklenburg to feed his army, and not the Berliners. But that was another point where he didn't see eye to eye with the Russian...

Fräulein von Sinnen started to sing a Zarah Leander song and the unpleasantness of Dean's day dissipated. Mesmerized by her extraordinary voice he hung on every note and wished he could spend his days with her, instead of battling General Sokolov at the Kommandatura.

After her performance he asked the waitress to send her a bottle of champagne with his compliments and the question whether she would be willing to join him at this table.

The waitress returned with a polite refusal and later he saw Fräulein von Sinnen leave the nightclub in the company of Captain Orlovski. Another Russian he wished to send packing.

CHAPTER 10

Werner leaned back in his chair in his – now fully furnished – office at the university building. They had been swamped with applications, but they'd had to reject almost two thirds of the applicants.

It was officially to weed out Nazis, but Norbert had soon told him to give preference to members of the communist and social-democratic parties, because students vetted in line with Soviet interests would prevent possible trouble later on.

The growing dissatisfaction of the Berliners with their Soviet occupiers had been a frequent discussion among the Gentner group and Werner was one of the few who promoted a more lenient and amiable treatment of the Germans to build a resilient relationship based on trust rather than fear. But most everyone else, including Norbert, favored the solution of doling out favors to politically reliable people while basically excluding the rest from public life – just like the Nazis had done.

Even though Werner feared that the Soviet policies would

lead down a slippery slope to something resembling the fascist regime they all hated, he never mentioned this to anyone.

After the warning issued by General Sokolov he meticulously guarded his tongue and never uttered a single word of criticism about whatever directive came his way. Even Norbert had praised him for his behavior and called him a model communist.

So why was Werner so annoyed with himself? He suspected he knew the reason, but was too cowardly to admit it, even to himself. Once upon a time he had been a hopeful and enthusiastic student, believing in the cause and the merits of communism – a people's revolution that brought wealth, freedom and appreciation for everyone.

Right now, he wasn't so sure anymore. The fruitful discourse about theories and policies he so enjoyed was all but nonexistent these days. Actually, in hindsight, a true discourse had never happened. The professors in Moscow had indulged the students in playing devil's advocate as long as the devil's arguments were inherently flawed, and in the end, everyone came to the conclusion that Stalin was always right.

He scoffed. Phony discussions! Young and malleable people led by experienced men, until the students completely stopped thinking for themselves. Shamefully he had to admit he'd fallen prey to the same pretentious omniscience – until he came to Berlin and experienced real life. Things were not the way Moscow wanted everyone to believe.

Werner winced at the memory of the beautiful brunette nurse glaring at him with her expressive eyes and yelling at him that he was a Soviet monster, forcing his filthy propaganda on her people.

And she wasn't wrong. From the moment General Sokolov had inaugurated *Rundfunk Berlin*, the new radio station, with the words, *"Hier spricht Berlin"*, this is Berlin speaking, all the radio did was twist the truth, propagate blatant lies, report biased or outright false news, and vilify the Americans. All of this in an attempt to assuage the Berliners' hate for their Soviet oppressors with sweet words.

A knock on the door ended his musings. A familiar-looking man in his late twenties entered the office, but Werner couldn't put a name or location to the face.

"*Guten Tag*, Herr Böhm, I'm Georg Tauber," the man said, handing him his student application. Werner was sure he'd never heard the name before, but the face was strangely familiar.

"Please sit down." He motioned at the chair in front of his desk and leafed through the application form. "You want to study medicine?"

"Yes, Herr Böhm."

"Do you have any previous experience?" He glanced at the young man with the curly brown hair, who was about his own age.

"Actually, yes. I studied four semesters of medicine here in Berlin before the war." Georg Tauber seemed unsure whether he should offer more information, so Werner prodded him, "Please continue and give me a short summary of what happened since."

"In 1941 the Nazis drafted me and sent me to the Eastern Front. After my return I wasn't allowed to continue my studies, because I refused to join the Nazi party. You must know, I was a member of the Christian Democratic Party."

Werner's ears perked up. "What happened then?"

"Well," Georg smirked. "The Nazis assigned me to work in an armaments factory, but they weren't at all pleased to find out that I told people about the atrocities committed at the Eastern Front. Before I knew, I was on my way to the Mauthausen concentration camp, where American troops

69

liberated me earlier this year. Just recently I returned to Berlin and am now helping a doctor with his patients."

Werner glanced at the two Russian guards in the corners of the office. It was a policy to never let anyone speak alone with people who weren't proven politically reliable. Although he doubted the guards understood a lot of German.

"That is quite the impressive anti-fascist biography you have here. I would like to suggest you for the student board. We need valiant anti-fascists like you for the denazification process. And I can't think of a better suited man for this position than you, a courageous man who opposed the Nazis from the very beginning regardless of the personal consequences."

"Thank you, Herr Böhm. It would be an honor for me to serve on the student board."

Werner was pleased. "I'll let my superior know. Would you please wait outside?"

As soon as Georg Tauber had left, Werner glanced at his wristwatch. It was already early afternoon. While Werner preferred to work during German office hours, Norbert had adopted the Russian habit of not showing up before noon.

He picked up the phone and called Norbert's office. "*Guten Tag*, Comrade Norbert. I have just interviewed an applicant who turns out to be a camp survivor and I should like you to have a word with him. He would be a perfect candidate for the student board."

"Is he a communist?"

"No, he's a Christian Democrat." Even through the phone Werner *saw* Norbert's face scrunching up and he hurried to add, "He is a convinced anti-fascist and as you said yourself, we have to make our institutions look democratic for the sake of the other Allies. Therefore, I believed it to be a good idea to have a few non-communists on the student board for good measure."

"Hmm...that is actually quite clever, Werner. You have learned your lesson well. I am glad your little chat with General Sokolov has put your head straight."

Werner gave a sour smile. "Will you want to talk to him?"

"Yes, please have him come to my office in an hour."

"Thank you." Werner disconnected the call and asked the Russian guard to order Herr Tauber inside. Then he said, "Herr Tauber, my boss Norbert Gentner would like to meet you and discuss the further process directly with you."

Werner gave the other man directions to Norbert's office in Prinzenallee 80 and said, "I hope to welcome you to the student board soon." Then he waved the next waiting applicant into his office.

The afternoon progressed and Werner grew curious as to whether Georg Tauber had passed the test. If the young man turned out to be a toad, Norbert would rub it in until the end of his days. On the other hand, the moment Norbert approved the nomination, the responsibility was taken from Werner's hands. Sometimes playing by the rules was comforting.

Late in the evening, after processing several dozen prospective students, he finally took his hat and briefcase and locked the door behind him. Just as he was stepping onto the street, a car stopped at the curb and Norbert stepped out, which was quite unusual.

"You weren't already leaving, were you?" Norbert asked.

Werner sighed. The Russians habitually turned night into day and rarely woke up before noon, but he adhered to the German nine-to-five schedule, although in his case it more often than not was nine-to-nine. "In fact, I was, because I interviewed prospective students for the past twelve hours."

Norbert didn't address the issue and instead said, "Get into my car." Once both of them settled in the back of the car, Norbert ordered the driver to take them to the Café de Paris

71

and then said, "About Georg Tauber, he's a great find. One hundred percent anti-fascist and hates the Nazis with a passion. He believes in a social democracy and has the potential to become a great leader."

Werner's soul warmed with pride. Tauber was his find, and if he became an asset to the communist party, it would strengthen Werner's own position.

"...but his Christian affiliations might pose a problem. You know what Stalin thinks about religion."

Naturally, he did and nodded.

"So, I want you to become friendly with him, keep an eye on him, make sure he knows which loyalties are in his best interest." Norbert looked utterly pleased with himself. Werner, not so much. Befriending a German wasn't usually encouraged by the Soviet administration. After all, they were the underlings.

"If this is your wish, I will certainly befriend him," Werner said, suddenly feeling a heavy burden on his chest. Thankfully, they reached the Café de Paris within minutes and he decided to follow the Russian model and drink himself into oblivion.

CHAPTER 11

Zara had fully recovered and Dr. Ebert told her she couldn't stay at the hospital any longer, because the bed was needed for other patients.

"What shall I do?" she asked Marlene.

"I'm so sorry. You know that I can't invite you to stay at our place, because my parents would never allow this." Marlene wrinkled her forehead in deep thought. "We could ask Bruni."

"Bruni? Over my dead body! She's living with that Russian captain, right?" Zara was trembling with fear.

Marlene looked at her friend with empathy. Zara had yet to overcome the traumatic shock. "She's not living with him...but he's visiting on a regular basis."

"I will not set foot into the same apartment with one of those depraved monsters," Zara said, pressing her lips into a tight line.

"I'll ask her if she knows of another place for you. You know Bruni, she has connections everywhere." From Zara's helpless shrug Marlene knew that she didn't like the idea, but wasn't in a position to be too proud to ask Bruni for help.

After finishing work, Marlene rushed off into the French sector, where Bruni lived. Her friend opened the door, dressed in a glittery, full-length gown other women could only dream about. Marlene's mouth hung agape and for a moment she couldn't form a single word.

"What a surprise!" Bruni hugged her, expensive perfume lingering in the air. "How are you?"

"Couldn't be better," Marlene replied with a shrug. Complaining about the awful living conditions in Berlin made them only worse.

Bruni laughed out loud. "Sweetie, I'm running late for work. Come with me? Then we can chat."

Marlene agreed. Together they walked to the Café de Paris. Marlene had never been inside a nightclub, but she'd heard plentiful rumors. It wasn't a place for decent women to go. Her heart beat faster and involuntarily she closed the buttons of her coat despite the warm evening.

Bruni picked up on her uneasiness and said, "Don't worry about it. You're safe with me."

Sometimes Marlene wondered where Bruni got her exceptional self-assuredness. She was so different from everyone else, and while many people found her selfish and superficial, Marlene knew her to have a big heart for her friends.

They entered the nightclub and went backstage to the dressing rooms. As soon as Bruni settled in front of the huge brightly lit mirror and used an eyelash curler on her long lashes, Marlene blurted out, "Zara needs a place to live."

Bruni left her arm hanging mid-air, before she continued her beauty program and stared at Marlene through the mirror. "You're not expecting me to take her in, are you?"

"Actually, this was what I was hoping for." Marlene didn't mention that Zara had already declined this possibility.

"Not on any account. Feodor would never approve." Bruni

completed her eyelash-curling and continued with painting her plucked eyebrows into a perfect curve.

"You need his permission to have a friend stay over?"

"Of course I don't. But he's arranged for the apartment, so I'd rather not upset him. Besides, how would we go at it with Zara around?"

Marlene felt the blood rushing to her face. She still couldn't wrap her head around the fact that Bruni was basically selling her body for food, shelter and clothing.

"Just for a few days, until I find something else. Please," Marlene begged.

"Wasn't her father commandant at Mauthausen?" Bruni pursed her lips to apply a bright red lipstick – another remnant of a more glorious past not many women in Berlin possessed.

"Yes, but what does this have to do with her?" Marlene was getting angry.

"It's just that she wouldn't be safe at my place. Not if Feodor finds out. The Russians strongly believe in clan liability and would whisk her away to a prison faster than you can blink. And before you cry murder, there's nothing Feodor can do about it. He's just a captain." Bruni made a sad face, as if suddenly regretting her choice of male companion, then she smiled into the mirror and blew a kiss. "But I'll ask around."

Marlene sighed.

"Don't look so sad. Why don't you and Zara visit my performance one day? I promise, we'll have a lot of fun."

"Thanks, Bruni, we'll certainly stop by."

"If you ever change your opinion about morals, I can introduce you and Zara to a couple of handsome officers," Bruni generously offered.

"Thanks. But no thanks."

"You're missing out big time. I gotta go." Bruni laughed and finished the make-up on her face. "See you soon."

Marlene shook her head. As much as she loved her friend, she hoped Bruni would one day grow up and take life seriously. Maybe if she found a man who truly loved her, she'd stop using them for her own ends. On her walk home, Marlene grew increasingly desolate. What should she do if she couldn't convince her parents to let Zara stay with them?

As she had feared, her parents would hear nothing of it. Her mother was adamant and her father ended the discussion with one sentence. "I will not allow this woman to enter my house ever again."

Marlene was close to tears. Wasn't there any kindness left in this world?

That night she was plagued by nightmares and woke up in the morning feeling like she had been run over by a train. She snatched a piece of bread from the small table they used as a kitchen and fled from the oppressive presence of her parents, whom she didn't understand anymore. She couldn't fathom their transformation from caring people into the whining stonehearted complainers they had become.

Two blocks from the hospital, she met Georg and grumbled, "Morning."

"Hey, Marlene, you look awful," he said.

His honest remark made her laugh despite herself. "That's because I slept like hell. Dr. Ebert has said Zara must leave the hospital, but she has nowhere to go. Even my parents refuse to let her stay with us."

Georg's brown eyes became pensive. "I could ask my cousin. She's living in the American sector and I'm sure she would take in your friend. But I have to warn you, her place is in a shambles."

"Which place isn't?" Marlene asked, her heart suddenly much lighter.

"Even by war standards it's an awful place to live in." They had reached the hospital and he opened the heavy door for her.

"I'm sure Zara won't mind. As long as it has a roof and four walls she'll be fine."

"Then let's go and tell her."

Marlene flinched. "Shouldn't you ask your cousin first?"

"No. She'd never turn down someone in need, and Zara's a friend." Georg's smile brightened the place and warmed Marlene's soul.

She instantly loved his cousin. And him by affiliation.

CHAPTER 12

T he friendship with Georg was getting along as planned. In fact, Werner liked the other man a lot. Georg was intelligent, a good conversational partner, had humor, loathed the Nazis and possessed natural authority.

Although they were the same age, Werner often saw in Georg his younger self, before disillusionment about the upcoming proletarian revolution had taken possession of him. Compared to the idealistic Georg, Werner was but an ancient cynic.

He shrugged. *Realist, not cynic. The revolutionary heat of the youth has to be guided by real-life experience.* Catching up to his inner dialogue, Werner broke out into a fit of hilarious giggles. *What kind of man is telling himself party propaganda -- and expecting him to believe it?* He shook his head, preferring to occupy his thoughts with Georg rather than with his own deficiencies.

The other students looked up at Georg for guidance. With just a little re-education, he'd be a valuable asset to the long-term plan of molding a unified communist student board.

Because, whatever Norbert and the others still *might* believe about Stalin's wish for a demilitarized and democratic Germany, Werner had come to the conclusion that it was nothing but a midsummer dream. Too big were the cultural differences between the Soviet way and the Western way. A peaceful coexistence wasn't possible.

Several days later, he and Georg were on their way back to university after visiting with an American education official in the American sector.

"It went quite well, the meeting," Werner said, when two visibly drunk Russian soldiers approached a German Fräulein with the words *Komm Frau*. Instinctively Werner turned his head, as he wanted nothing to do with their shameful behavior.

But Georg elbowed him, "They are going to rape her. You need to do something."

"There's nothing I can do," Werner said, hot waves of shame coursing through his body. Both of them knew that as a German citizen Georg wasn't allowed to interfere with an Allied soldier, whereas Werner technically belonged to the occupying force.

"But you are a Soviet government official!" Georg exclaimed.

"I may be, but I am not a Red Army member. These men obey only orders from above." Werner looked away as the two Russians grabbed the girl by her arms and dragged her across the pavement into a nearby building. At least they wouldn't do their ghastly business out in the open where everyone could watch, and humiliate the poor woman even more.

"You measly coward! I won't stand by and watch." Georg yelled at Werner and ran off. Despite knowing better, Werner rushed behind his friend. After about a block Georg came across a group of Americans and shouted breathlessly, "Rape. Russian. There."

The GIs were all too familiar with such unfortunate occurrences and despite Georg's bad English, it didn't take them longer than a few seconds to react and run in the direction Georg indicated.

Werner pointed wordlessly at the building where the Russians had taken their victim, but preferred not to follow them inside. He argued with himself whether he should stay and wait or quietly disappear. Nothing good ever came out of getting involved.

While he pondered the best course of action to take, several shots rang through the air and made his predicament even more precarious. *Damn Georg for getting the Americans involved.*

He certainly didn't want to be caught up in a diplomatic turmoil, and furtively glanced around before he took his leave and disappeared into the next underground station. The entire way home, he had a nagging feeling that this incident would have consequences. Since he couldn't risk being connected to a Russian encroachment in the American sector, he needed an alibi. The first-best thing he could think of was the Café de Paris.

The smoke-filled nightclub was buzzing with uniformed men. Werner was glad of the crowd. His eyes narrowed as he peered around, looking for a familiar face to back his alibi. Beautiful women abounded, and the unattached females tried to vie for a position on the arm of an officer or a gentleman, especially one as handsome as this tall blond man who had just entered the room.

Werner was not interested when they zeroed in on him, and he continued to scan the place for someone he knew. There was a resounding sound of applause for the singer who'd stepped onto the small stage. In the glare of a spotlight, Werner spied Captain Orlovski with a group of officers, and squeezed through the crush of bodies, making his way over to their table.

"Ah, Comrade Böhm, you're not leaving, are you?" Orlovski asked.

"I've been here for almost an hour, but my colleagues needed to attend another party," he lied.

"Their loss. The evening has just begun. Please sit with us," Orlovski said.

"Thank you, Comrade Orlovski, it would be a pleasure," Werner fell into one of the plush seats next to Orlovski, who introduced him to his two colleagues. The singer on the stage was announced as "the amazing chanteuse Fräulein von Sinnen".

The moment she began her first chanson, the teeming place fell completely silent, every man in the room mesmerized by her beauty and her impressive voice. When she ended the song, deafening applause filled the place. During the short break, a young waitress arrived. "Champagne?"

"Yes, please."

One of the officers in his group guffawed. "The pansy's saying please, hear that? The *Fräuleins* here prefer a more hands-on attitude." To emphasize his words, he squeezed the waitress's ass.

Werner dutifully joined in the rowdy laughter, despite the nagging voice inside scolding him for being such a sycophant.

After her performance, the singer stepped down from the stage, gracefully accepting the thundering applause and throwing kisses into the crowd. Her figure-hugging green gown with delicate fine straps clinging to her smooth shoulders turned heads as she came directly toward their table, dismissing over-eager men with a simple raising of her brow and a scathing glance.

"Bruni," Orlovski stood up, his eyes shining with pride as

the singer kissed him on the cheeks and graciously accepted a glass of champagne. "May I introduce you to Werner Böhm, responsible for education and culture in the city administration."

She stretched out a perfectly manicured, slender hand. "It's my pleasure, Herr Böhm."

Werner dutifully stood up and kissed the back of her hand. "I'm impressed by your talent. You have a voice one will not easily forget."

She smiled at him and then took her place next to Orlovski, leaving Werner wondering just how intimate the two of them were.

"How's that university doing?" Orlovski asked, pouring more champagne into the half-empty glasses.

"Going along well, thanks to your kind intervention." Werner looked at Fräulein von Sinnen and said, "The captain here rescued me from quite the predicament."

Between chitchat, more champagne, and plenty of vodka, the time passed, and it was after midnight when two more Soviets arrived.

"Why so late?" one of the officers at Werner's table slurred, beckoning the newcomers to sit down.

"Fucking Americans, sticking their noses into our business," Petrov, the burly one with a thick Stalin-like mustache, said.

"What have they done now?" Orlovski asked, downing the last of his vodka and signaling for another bottle.

Petrov gasped. "Yes, what? They have only shot dead two of our soldiers on trumped-up charges!"

"Shot? Trumped-up charges?" Werner didn't need to act to show his shock. He couldn't be sure they were talking about the same incident that had happened earlier this afternoon, but it was very likely.

Fräulein von Sinnen rolled her eyes at him as if saying "You don't fool me with your phony agitation." Then she whispered something into Orlovski's ear and returned to the stage. This time her lovely voice was drowned out at Werner's table as the men heatedly discussed the murder of two innocent Russian soldiers by the vile and aggressive Americans.

Werner listened silently while the others were livid at the outrage. That the Russian soldiers had been caught in the act of raping a German girl was not a matter of concern, whereas the shooting stirred fierce indignation among the men.

"Do we walk around shooting Americans? No! So, what right do these assholes have? Wicked imperialist devils!" Petrov slammed his fist on the table.

"And for what? I'll bet that German slut has done it before, probably with the whole brigade!"

"Right! Since when do the Germans have rights all of a sudden? We're the conquerors and we can do as we please." Petrov was talking himself into a rage, and even the whores in the nightclub, who normally clung to every unattached man, retreated from the vicinity of their table.

"Didn't you say it happened in the American sector?" Werner interjected in the hopes of cooling down the exuberant emotions. "It's not the first time the Americans have issued a warning that they won't allow these things in their sector."

The men erupted in a roar of disapproval and anger, hotly disagreeing with his statement.

"Are you a friend of the imperialists, Böhm?" Bagrov, a red-faced officer, retorted. "Perhaps you are the one who reported our soldiers to the Americans."

"What an insulting thing to say to a comrade," Werner shot back, standing up and making ready to leave.

"Come on, men, take it easy," Orlovski said. "We have enough enemies without turning on our own."

Bagrov growled, "Easy for you to say, for the shot comrade

wasn't your brother." A shocked silence ensued and Werner feared the man could look right through him and find out that he'd been there. He hadn't personally told on the now-dead soldiers, but he hadn't prevented Georg from doing so. Either way he was as good as dead should Bagrov ever find out.

"I swear I'll tear the informer apart with my bare hands. Collaborating with the Americans to shoot our war heroes."

"To move forward, we might find something to learn from this incident," Werner said, though he knew he should probably retire for the night on the excuse that he was exhausted, which he was. Physically and mentally.

"Learning from a cold-blooded murder?" Bagrov was getting heated again.

"The Americans have found a way to endear themselves to the German population by stopping the crimes and taking the local side," Werner said, keeping his cool and trying to explain his point of view to the drunken men. "This strategy works for them nicely, while we are hated more every day. Can't you see there is a lesson to be learned in this?"

"We must have no witnesses?" said Petrov, further dumbed down by the amount of alcohol he had consumed.

"This is the problem with intellectuals, they think too much," Bagrov said and the army officers burst out laughing. "Böhm, you should leave the problem to the army and stick to what you are assigned to do. Let's hope you can manage that well enough."

Werner was saved from giving an answer by the appearance of the beautiful Fräulein von Sinnen. She nodded in Orlovski's direction and the captain made his excuses to leave with his lady-love in tow. Werner got up as well, figuring he had spent enough time with these witnesses to ensure his defense.

CHAPTER 13

Dean was on his way to the Kommandatura, hoping General Sokolov was in an agreeable mood. The general suffered from peptic ulcers and on the days they were tormenting him, he returned the favor by abusing the other attendees at the Kommandatura meetings even more than usual.

Sometimes Dean wished he could solve the issue in the good old-fashioned manner with a blow to Sokolov's chin. But alas, the war was over and physical violence was frowned upon, at least in the US Army.

The first point on the agenda was the refugee problem. Berlin was in a shambles as it was, food scarce and housing hopeless. The influx of hundreds of thousands of German refugees expelled from Russia, Poland, and Czechoslovakia, along with returning Wehrmacht soldiers, further aggravated the food situation, and also the public-health problem. Many of the people arrived full of lice, sick of typhus, typhoid fever, tuberculosis and other contagious diseases.

The soldiers especially were a pathetic sight, and Dean's

heart constricted every time he saw one of them. He'd been enraged at the despicable treatment of his compatriot prisoners of war by the Nazis, but what the Russians had done to the German prisoners of war was on a par with the Nazi treatment.

Wretched, dirty, hollow-eyed, and scraggly men trudged into the capital wearing filthy, tattered uniforms, their only belonging – a tin cup – on a strap wrapped around their necks. And those were the healthy ones. The wounded, sick and injured hobbled on wooden splints and had grimy bandages wrapped around their heads, arms, or legs. Shoes were a rare sight and many of the soldiers had tied old newspapers, rags and wooden planks around their feet. Never in his life had Dean seen more dejected, defeated and desolate soldiers. Abysmal despair.

Dean had a few ideas about what could be done to discourage people from coming to Berlin, and trying their luck in the less crowded smaller towns and villages instead.

The first measure, of not issuing staying permits, had not been very successful. He'd already said to his French and British colleagues that they needed to do something drastic. And now he hoped to convince General Sokolov to agree on a joint effort using a press and radio campaign throughout the Soviet zone, urging the refuges to stay away from Berlin and warning them that disease and hunger would be their only welcome.

But as he arrived at the Kommandatura, the refugee problem was brushed aside by a livid Sokolov insisting on addressing a more pressing immediate emergency – the cold-blooded murder of two of his men in the American sector the afternoon before.

Dean inwardly groaned. It wasn't the first time this had happened, and it certainly wouldn't be the last if those bloody

Russians didn't start to discipline and control their troops. He glanced at his deputy Major Gardner, who'd already requested the police report and caught Dean up on the topic. An attempted rape, a German informer, two American military police coming to aid the girl, and two insolent Russians who'd threatened them with a gun.

It would be a long day.

Sokolov began with his usual hateful tirade against the Western imperialists and then demanded satisfaction by having the murderer handed over to Soviet jurisdiction. Obviously, everyone in the room knew this was an absolute no-go, but Sokolov probably used it to make his point: the lack of cooperation from the Americans in dispensing justice.

"General Sokolov, I'm afraid your facts are entirely wrong," Gardner said and began reading the details of the incident from the police report. Sokolov's face became increasingly convulsed with anger, and Dean secretly hoped he'd burst asunder in the midst, gushing out his bowels.

"So maybe they had a few drinks and stepped over the line. That's no reason to shoot our men," Sokolov conceded.

"We usually don't shoot your men either, but in this case the Russians drew their weapons first and threatened our people," Gardner said.

Sokolov looked thoroughly uncomfortable. "Well, you should know that this was only symbolic, they never intended to actually kill your men."

Dean had difficulties suppressing a laugh. He'd recently come to the conclusion that this was the fundamental difference between the two armies. In an altercation with the Western Allies, the Russians usually drew their weapons to threaten or impress, and often fired warning shots, if they fired at all. An American soldier, though, only drew his weapon to shoot, and if he fired, he did it to kill.

"General, you must agree that our men couldn't know this and fired in self-defense," Gardner replied.

"Your people shouldn't have interfered with our business in the first place," Sokolov raged.

Dean had heard enough. He stood and said, "With all due respect, General, but what happens in our sector is our business. You can't expect us to allow your people to rape, loot and shoot without wanting to stop them."

There wasn't much that Sokolov could bring up against Dean's argument. Despite the quadripartite ruling of Berlin, each power had full control over her respective sector. And the Russians were the first ones to tell the others to keep their noses out of the Soviet sector.

"The British have never shot one of our soldiers," Sokolov accused.

The French commandant entered the discussion, "That's because the British much prefer to beat your people to a pulp."

"See, the British know how to deal with insolent soldiers, while you Americans always have to use excessive violence." As always, Sokolov must have the last word. At least he dropped the issue and agreed to work on the meeting agenda.

Dean just hoped that the Russians would understand that anyone caught murdering, looting or raping in the American sector might end up in a coffin and thus preferred to do their ugly deeds in their own sector from now on.

CHAPTER 14

January 1946

G eorg was delighted at the opportunity to continue his studies at the recently opened Berlin University. He still worked at Dr. Ebert's hospital during his free hours and never missed a chance to tell Marlene about the joys of being a student again even though he had to burn the midnight oil to keep up with his busy schedule.

"Why don't you enroll in classes, too, Marlene?" said Georg often enough to make the young woman sigh deeply.

"I don't know," she shrugged. "The last time I hit the books was before...well, it was quite some time ago. I'm quite happy at what I do."

"Don't sell yourself short," Georg protested. "Don't you have ambitions? You told me yourself that you'd love to become a lawyer instead of carrying law cases from one room to the next."

That much was true. Marlene had worked as a legal secretary for a family lawyer throughout the war, and once upon a time it had been her wish to study as well. "I would love to, but where's the time, Georg?" she moaned. "I'm exhausted as it is. And how will I earn money when I'm studying all day? No, that ship has sailed."

"Believe me, it was difficult for me in the beginning too, but now that I've organized my time, everything has fallen into place. I'm not saying it's easy, but the thought of getting my degree means the world to me. There's going to be a huge demand for skilled people and I want to be there to take my pick of opportunities."

"I'll think about it," she promised just to stop Georg from badgering her. She well remembered a time when she once had dreams too, before the chaos of war had altered her life and shattered her hopes.

"The opening ceremony is held a week from now," Georg said excitedly. "As chairman of the newly formed student board, I am allowed to give a speech. Please will you be my guest?"

"Of course, I'll be there. I'm so proud of you." She gave him a sisterly hug, looking forward to festivities that would interrupt the dullness of her life. The winter so far had been surprisingly mild, compared to the years before, but that only alleviated the worst of the problems. People were still hungry, cold, dull and desperate.

The inauguration of the Berlin University a week later was just as impressive as the Russians had planned. Marlene almost got the impression there was no shortage of food or other goods in her city. The first speech was held by Lord Mayor Arthur Werner, a respectable man with white hair and the most impeccable appearance. He'd run a private technical college until the Nazis forced him to retire in 1942. Every Berliner liked him and valued his genuine interest in helping his fellow Berliners.

Marlene listened to Lord Mayor Werner's speech only with half an ear. It was widely known that he wielded little power. Installed as Lord Mayor because of his conciliatory conduct, the real power in the administration belonged to his deputy Karl Maron, a German communist from the Moscow-trained Gentner group. He was an intelligent but unscrupulous man who never thought twice about forcing Moscow's views onto the Berliners.

The next speaker was Werner Böhm, the rising star in the Berlin administration, newly appointed head of the Agitation and Propaganda department that not only controlled the press, but also the education system. He'd been the driving force behind the reopening of the university.

His pale face with the short blond hair constantly appeared in the newspapers and he always had an austere, even cantankerous air about him. She scrunched up her nose, because she still hadn't forgiven him for shutting down Dr. Ebert's hospital last summer to make room – as she later found out -- for a radio station, even though the move had turned out to be a godsend. The new building was much larger, with more amenities, and it stood under the protection of the Americans, who actually cared for the well-being of the Berliners.

Böhm's sonorous voice completely enthralled her and she found herself glued to his voice listening to every one of his words. Much to her surprise, he emphasized not only the great friendship between the Soviet and German people, but also his ambition for a first-class education system that included academic freedom and prolific political discourse. That was a clear deviation from the usual Soviet directive.

She studied his face and found it looked much friendlier than she remembered it, attractive even. His piercing eyes weren't the ones of a stone-hearted career politician, but of a staunch agent for a better future filled with health, wealth and freedom.

His speech launched a definite and contagious optimism in the air, and Marlene felt a twinge of envy at not being a part of this brave new generation trying to ensure bright prospects ahead for themselves and their country.

Wasn't it her duty to help rebuild her nation from the ashes? Shouldn't she bury the hatchet and step up to the task? If Herr Böhm could change, so could she. Because if she was honest with herself, she had to admit that a great part of her reluctance to enroll at university had been the very existence of Werner Böhm – the man she'd called a monster.

The last speech of the day was Georg's: a fervent plea for peace among the nations and academic freedom for students who sought to rebuild the country. When he finished, students, faculty and the inescapable military personnel alike applauded frantically.

People came up to congratulate him on his words, and Marlene beamed with pride to see how far her friend had come on the road to fulfilling his dreams for the future. When the crowd around him thinned, Georg scanned the room for Marlene and as soon as his eyes met hers, he made his way across the hall to greet her. Just a few steps away from her, Werner Böhm caught up to him.

"Well done." The tall, handsome man shook Georg's hand. "I have high hopes for you."

"You are too kind, Werner," Georg said modestly. "It is your support and encouragement that got me to where I am. I thank you for your attention and remain forever in your debt." Turning to Marlene, Georg said, "Marlene, this is my good friend Werner Böhm. Werner, this is Marlene Kupfer."

Marlene's mouth gaped open and she couldn't believe her own ears. The two men called each other by their first names?

Did Georg expect her to call the Soviet puppet by his first name, too? Thankfully, Böhm took the decision out of her hands.

He greeted her with a perfect kiss on the hand and his deep voice attracted her more than it should, "Fräulein Kupfer. It's my pleasure to meet such an attractive woman."

It wasn't her pleasure, though. "Herr Böhm, I was impressed by your speech today. Say, have the Soviets changed their official directives and suddenly support academic freedom?"

Georg gasped at the affront, but Böhm broke out in a chuckle. "I see you haven't forgiven me for my unfortunate role during our last encounter. I was only the messenger and I'm still heartbroken," he put a hand across his chest and looked at her with the most intense eyes, "at your calling me a vicious monster."

Now she felt like the worst person in the room. How did he do that?

But his ensuing smile betrayed his true feelings and despite herself, her heart warmed when he asked, "Please, how can I prove to you that I'm not the vicious monster you think I am?"

Marlene swallowed, hoping he hadn't noticed her inner turmoil, when Georg raised his voice. "Actually, I have tried to persuade Marlene to enroll for a degree. Maybe you could convince her to do so, Werner?"

"I would gladly do so. The university is severely lacking in intelligent and quick-witted young women, such as you. As you know, the Soviets foster the equality of all people, and strive for giving women the same rights as men." Werner cast her the most charming smile and for a moment she was swayed in her opinion. The handsome Herr Böhm behaved in such a considerate, charming and authentic way, could she have misjudged his character that badly? "Please, will you put in an application, and I promise I'll examine it myself."

"I...I'm really not sure..." she stammered, shrinking under his intense gaze. Considered attractive with her long brown hair and vivid blue eyes, men had always looked at her with leering eyes, but Herr Böhm's gaze was different. He seemed to actually be interested in her, and not only in her appearance. *Nonsense*, she scolded herself. *He simply wants you to enroll to reach his women's quota.*

"What subjects are you interested in, Fräulein Kupfer?" He persisted, his eyes holding her captive and reaching deep inside of her, into a part that she'd closed off after the Russian soldiers had taken what they considered their rightful reward for the hardships of war.

"Law," she replied, shrugging off the discomforting emotions attacking her. "I worked as a legal assistant for the past three years."

"As it happens, we are opening four more faculties, one of them law," Böhm smiled. "It would be a shame if you turned down such an opportunity to be in the front seat of history rebuilding your country. We need the likes of you, caring, unerring women who only answer to the law and honestly want to help their compatriots. Your friend Georg and I will support you all throughout the journey. What do you say, Georg?"

"Absolutely," Georg replied, eagerly. "I'll get the forms for you to fill out, Marlene."

"Will I have to take a test?" Marlene asked, nervously. Herr Böhm might consider her straightforward and courageous, but in truth she was shy and had always taken a back seat to her more assertive friends or brothers. An obedient daughter, she was at her best caring for others. Being cast into the spotlight frightened her and she longed to return to the familiarity and anonymity of Dr. Ebert's makeshift hospital.

"There is a screening process, but I'm sure any friend of Georg's won't have a problem," Böhm said, encouragingly. "We look for Nazi affiliations and criminal backgrounds. We also check for political attitudes and activities. I don't think you have anything to worry about."

Seeing her hesitation, he turned to Georg and said, "Help the lady out and see that she makes an appointment with my secretary for the screening as soon as possible, the classes are filling up faster than we anticipated."

A man in a Soviet military uniform beckoned to Herr Böhm and he gave a quick nod, before taking Marlene's hand into his to put a kiss on the back of it. "Duty calls, but I hope to see you soon, *schönes Fräulein*."

Marlene reeled from the compliment. Beautiful, he'd called her. He truly was a well-educated and charming gentleman, so unlike the other Russian brutes. But then, he was a born German, although his parents had emigrated to Moscow when he was but ten years old.

"This man is smitten with you," Georg said. "He could barely take his eyes off you."

"What an imagination you have." She tried to make light of what had transpired.

"Do I, really? Because the way I saw it, he wasn't alone in his infatuation. On the contrary, you did your bit to encourage him."

She gave a nervous giggle. "That's completely ridiculous. I was just being polite. Besides, I'd never fall for a communist."

CHAPTER 15

A few days later Marlene was surprised to get a call from Werner Böhm's office, informing her of the date and time for an appointment regarding her enrolment as a law student.

She rushed to the hospital, impatiently waiting for Georg to show up in between classes so she could give him the news. Elated and anxious at the same time, she went through the tasks that had become second nature to her during the past months – dressing wounds, changing bandages, washing patients or helping them to get out of bed. She did it out of a sense of duty, but unlike Georg and Dr. Ebert, the field of medicine wasn't her calling. She longed to return to the legal field, to an office filled with healthy people instead of the sick.

"Georg, can you imagine?" She all but barreled into her dearest friend in her hurry to tell him the good news.

"What is it that demands you attack me like a wild animal?" Georg smiled at her and she immediately felt a rush of guilt running up her spine. Her behavior wasn't exactly appropriate for a young lady.

"Herr Böhm has invited me for an admission interview two days from now."

"Now, that's good news. I'm so happy for you," he said, giving her a quick hug, before he let go of her and frowned. He'd been the one to push and encourage her, so she wondered what caused his discomfort.

"What's wrong?" she asked.

"Nothing…it's just…I don't want you to get hurt. Böhm is my mentor and he has been nothing but good to me, but… he is such a sophisticated man and clearly has set an eye on you."

Marlene felt herself blush and adamantly denied that she felt any attraction toward Werner Böhm. "Your fear is completely unfounded, or have you forgotten how he behaved when he closed down our hospital? I could never feel anything for a cold-hearted man like him."

"I remember that too," Georg admitted. "Werner was just doing his duty, since he was under strict orders to requisition the building that very day. After getting to know him I have nothing but compliments for him, he's far from the cold career politician everyone believes him to be. He's in fact an honest, intelligent and compassionate man."

Marlene shrugged, not understanding Georg's motives. First, he tried to warn her away from Böhm and now he kept singing his praises?

Georg must have seen her confusion and added, "I'm just worried about you. You're a wonderful, sweet girl, and he's a man of power. He does have to obey the party line and might hurt you without intending to."

"You're probably right," she murmured. Georg's opinion didn't help. He was a man and didn't understand her inner turmoil. She urgently needed female advice. And who better to give advice in romantic affairs than her friend Bruni?

In the evening she intercepted Bruni on her way to the Café de Paris.

"Can I talk to you?" Marlene asked.

"Sure, is it about a man?" Bruni linked arms with her and together they walked through the frosty evening.

"Why do you always assume there's a man behind everything?" Marlene exhaled and observed the white vapor coming from her mouth rising up into the air. The harsh cold seeped through her thin coat and she eyed Bruni's fur coat with envy.

"Because of the scarlet flush on your face, maybe?" Bruni laughed. Thankfully they soon arrived at the cabaret and the bouncer let them inside into the warmth. Most people heated their apartments sparsely, but since the nightclub catered primarily to Allied soldiers, it never suffered from a shortage of coal.

Marlene followed her friend to the tiny dressing room filled with glamorous gowns, feather boas, hats, and dozens of cosmetic products. Never short of extravagances, Bruni opened a bottle of fine wine and poured both of them a glass, before she seated herself in front of the oversized, lit-up mirror.

"Spill the beans," Bruni demanded, scrutinizing her friend's face in the mirror as she outlined her perfect mouth with a deep red lipstick.

Marlene took a deep breath, wondering whether it had been a mistake to come for advice. She already knew what Bruni would say. "It's about Werner Böhm."

"*The* Werner Böhm?" Bruni's eyes widened and she took a sip of the dark red wine, leaving a mark of her equally dark red lipstick on the glass.

"Yes, him, one of the Gentner group." Suddenly aware that Böhm was one of the ten most powerful Germans in Berlin, she shuddered. She was way in over her head. No, no, and no.

Even indulging the idea of a romantic relationship with him was out of the question.

"He's quite the handsome chap," Bruni said.

"Right? And he's so much more impressive in real life than in the newspapers." Marlene couldn't stop babbling. "He's a true gentleman with perfect manners. His presence is so...so... overwhelming, and his charming smile. Oh, but...his voice! You have to hear his voice. It's nothing like on the radio, it draws you right in like some magnetic force."

"Dear God! You have it bad for him," Bruni said and twirled around on her stool to look directly into Marlene's eyes.

"I don't," Marlene weakly protested.

Bruni took no notice and said, "So, now you're asking for my advice on how to attract his attention, right?"

"Not at all." Marlene forcefully shook her head, her brown wavy hair swooshing around. "I'd rather know how to dodge his attraction."

"You what?" Bruni set down her glass, giving her friend a stern look. "You come here to tell me the most coveted civilian bachelor in all of Berlin has the hots for you and want me to tell you how to get rid of him? Is that right?"

"Hmm...yes. Or maybe not...I mean...I..." Marlene sighed. "He wants me to enroll in law school and has personally invited me to the interview. I guess I wanted to know whether this was a good idea or not."

"You must be kidding me. Every other girl would kill for his attention and you're asking me whether this is a good idea."

"I'm not every other girl." Marlene itched to leave this place. It definitely had been a mistake to ask for Bruni's advice. But her friend was in her element and started a long monologue about the benefits of having a protector in these dire times.

"Having a man like Werner Böhm fancy you is the best thing that could happen to you. Don't you see this? He's handsome, charming, decent. Böhm is just the sort of chap to attract. Being the object of his desires is like winning a lottery. That man can help you in all manner of ways. He can get you things nobody else in Berlin has. Go for it, I say!"

"Oh, Bruni, it's not about things."

"It is. We all want to survive and for that we need things: food, warm clothes, a roof above our heads. Add to that an accomplished man in your bed and what more could you ask for?" Bruni turned back toward the mirror and put blue eye shadow on her lids.

"Love?" A nostalgic emotion surged in Marlene, as she remembered the sweet first love with her late fiancé. A pure and warm feeling, that had nothing to do with material benefits.

"Love is overrated," Bruni scoffed. "Men are inherently disloyal and selfish. You take from them whatever you can get and when they inevitably tire of you, you move on to the next one. That's how life really is. Love is just a ruse the Nazis invented to make you produce dozens of little crying babies for the Führer."

Marlene felt sorry for her friend, who'd never experienced true love in her life. Not from her estranged parents and certainly not from one of her lovers. But it wouldn't do good to launch into an argument about love right now. "Böhm's a communist, a career politician. He has a dark side to him. Remember I told you how our hospital was emptied? It was him who did this."

"All men have different facets to their characters." Bruni looked at her handiwork in the mirror, pouting her lips to see the effect. "So do women, for that matter. Böhm is interested, you have a chance at getting a degree, if you don't take full advantage of this deal, you're an idiot."

"Ouch! Is this the best advice you can give me?" Marlene was on the verge of tears.

"Yes," Bruni said drily, refilling their glasses with the rest of the Pinot Noir. "If you don't take it, you're a bigger fool than I thought."

"I don't know..." Marlene said dolefully.

"I think you do know, Marlene," Bruni replied pointedly. "The fact that you have come to me for advice and not to Zara clearly shows what you wanted to hear."

~

On the day of her interview Marlene dressed carefully, wearing her best dress and even using a bit of make-up, which she'd borrowed from Bruni. Happiness gave her an added sparkle and she arrived at the university, her completed application forms pressed to her chest.

Frau Busch, Böhm's secretary, took them and asked her to wait in the hallway outside until one of the law professors became available. The words took a load off her mind and she scolded herself for reading too much into Böhm's charming smile. But at once a confusing twinge of disappointment seared through her. It's not that she wanted him to fancy her. Hell, she certainly didn't fancy him.

When Frau Busch returned to call her inside, she said, "Herr Böhm will personally conduct your interview."

Emotions surged through her veins and she could only give a faint nod. What on earth had led him to change the standard process and attend to her himself? She frantically searched for a mouse hole to disappear into, but of course, this was impossible. Steeling her spine, she plastered a smile on her face and entered the office.

"Ah, good morning Fräulein Kupfer," he said brightly. "I wouldn't want to miss out on revising your application personally." Then he explained to a rail-thin man with completely white hair sitting at the side of the desk, "Professor Klein, this is Marlene Kupfer, a very promising student. She was recommended by Georg Tauber, the chair of our student board."

Professor Klein removed the glasses he'd been using to read her application form and observed her with a piercing glance. Despite the friendly expression on his face, Marlene felt intimidated. Professor Klein was one of the most distinguished law experts in all of Germany and even the Nazis hadn't dared to touch him, albeit after having advised him to stay out of politics.

She had somehow expected to be asked about her legal background and any prior experience in the field that might qualify her to become a law student, but instead the professor asked question after question about the professions and political opinions of her family and herself.

Her answers were as stereotypical as the scripted questions. "Yes, Professor, I was a member of the BDM, the German Girls Union," and, "No, Professor, I wasn't an NSDAP party member. No, I'm not a member of a church nor of a political party."

All through the inquisition she nervously rubbed her sweaty palms against her dress and tried not to look in Böhm's direction, because his first encouraging smile had done nothing to ease her anxiety. On the contrary, her stomach had fluttered violently.

"Fräulein Kupfer, would you please elaborate on your vision for a new Berlin?" Herr Böhm asked.

She couldn't avoid looking at him, and the way his eyes intensely closed in on hers turned her knees to jelly and set an army of butterflies fluttering in her stomach. Quickly turning to Professor Klein, she found strength in his stern, wrinkled face and somehow managed to say, "I wish for a peaceful co-existence of the Germans with the Allies. And I should hope that with time Berliners will regain ownership over our administration and we can live in a truly democratic and lawful state."

"Very well said, Fräulein Kupfer." Böhm beamed with enthusiasm and stood up. His physical presence was overpowering, and she wished at the same time to flee from the room and have him trap her in his embrace.

Naturally, neither of the two things happened. Instead he stepped out from behind his desk, taking two steps toward her and starting a speech about the Soviet intention of building a democratic German state, the necessity of political parties and the freedom of speech, the principles of democracy, the foundation of a state in a constitution and a proper jurisdiction.

Marlene felt his need to express the good intentions of the Soviets and she was mesmerized by the passion with which he declaimed the arguments – until he praised the Red Army for their crucial part in liberating Berlin from the Nazi evil.

It was then that she tore her gaze away from him and found Professor Klein's eyes, which mirrored her own disdain for the Russian soldiers. But neither of them uttered a word of protest.

Böhm's speech came to a glorious end praising Berlin's paradisiacal conditions in a not so distant future under the beneficial rule of socialism. Then he looked at Professor Klein and said, "I'm sure you'll agree with me, that this bright young lady here is accepted into the university."

"Certainly," Professor Klein said. He must be well aware of the hierarchy in the room. If the Soviet-installed chairman of the Culture and Education department deemed a student worthy to be enrolled at the law faculty, a law professor had no further say in the matter. "Classes begin next month. Frau Busch will give you the details."

Later that day Marlene met with her friends Zara and Bruni, giddy to bring them the good news.

"So, tell us the juicy news," Bruni greeted her with a huge grin.

"How do you know there's news?" Marlene stuttered, but she knew she couldn't deceive her friends. Shy Zara would never open a conversation like this, but of course Bruni cut right to the chase.

"Isn't it true that you've been pining for Werner Böhm, since the university inauguration?" Bruni laughed.

"And I hear he's crazy about you," Zara added.

"Who told you this?" Marlene eyed the two of them with a suspicious glance.

"Georg's cousin of course. Herr Böhm talks about nothing but you when he's alone with Georg," Zara answered.

Good gracious. Just what Marlene needed. Even before she joined the university, she already was the center of gossip.

"And…is it true? Are you and Böhm a thing?" Bruni asked.

"Don't rush her, you know she'll tell us in time," Zara, the voice of reason in their trio, said. Her amazing waist-length hair astounded everyone with its ebony shimmer that contrasted perfectly with her porcelain skin and her red lips, making her look like a real-life version of Snow White.

"I have decided that Böhm isn't for me, but…" Marlene found pleasure in keeping her friends on tenterhooks. She took a measured sip from the wine glass Bruni handed her. The full aroma attacked her senses and she inhaled deeply to smell more of the heavy, fruity scent. With an evil smile toward Bruni, she said, "That wine is delicious. Truly special."

"Enough prevarication. I have to leave soon." Bruni couldn't hide the fact that she was dying to hear Marlene's news.

"If you insist…I've been accepted into law school today."

Zara threw her arms around Marlene, hugging her tight. "That's such great news. When will you start?"

"Next month already," Marlene beamed with pride, completely forgetting how reluctant she's been to apply at the university.

"I'm happy to see you optimistic like this." Zara smiled. "Joining the university is a great move. A law degree will ensure a comfortable future."

"It's all well and good to plan for the future," Bruni said with pursed lips, putting a damper on Marlene's elation. "But what about the present? Who will provide for you and pay your bills? Certainly not your parents."

"I've been thinking about this myself...I could still work with Dr. Ebert between classes the way Georg does."

"That's what I mean," Bruni replied. "You'll be spreading yourself thin, working at that place and studying at the same time. How long do you think you'll last under such pressure?"

Marlene sighed. "I don't know."

"It won't be forever," Zara said. "As soon as Marlene is settled, she can go looking for a job in the legal field. Maybe even at the university, something where she can combine work and study. Aren't you happy for her? Remember it was you who encouraged her to pursue this opportunity."

"Oh no, don't put this on me." Bruni raised an eyebrow in an effort to look offended. "My advice was to take advantage of Böhm's attention and start her studies with the comfortable knowledge that he will provide for her. Now that silly woman has bitten the hand that wants to feed her. How will she put food on the table and clothes on her back?"

Zara and Bruni were arguing back and forth on her behalf, until Marlene had had enough and stomped her foot on the floor. "Hey! I'm still here."

A perplexed Bruni broke out into a giggle. "Yes, sweetie,

you are. And you know that I'll always support you, but my support includes some tough love. Zara here might be too chicken to tell you, but someone's gotta spring the truth on you. You're missing out on a once-in-a-lifetime opportunity by not entertaining Böhm's attraction."

"I know. But unlike you I actually value love, and he simply isn't the man for me." Marlene sighed and her eyes became dreamy at the memory of his intense gaze and the electric tension she always felt in his presence. If he were any other man but a leading communist party official... No, she simply could not allow herself to have feelings for him.

"What's not to love about him?" Bruni was about to start another lecture in how to deal with men, but closed her mouth when Zara interrupted her with a warning glare. "Have I told you about my new job as a kitchen aide in the French casern?"

Marlene jumped on the new topic like a drowning person on a lifeline and said, "That's wonderful. Tell us all about it. Is the French cuisine as delicious as they say?"

Food was a predominant topic among the Berliners, especially the shortage of it. Talking about French delicacies was almost as good as actually eating them, and it eased the tension among the three friends.

When they finally parted, they hugged each other tightly. Despite their different outlooks on life, their friendship was deep and strong, and Marlene knew she could always count on Bruni and Zara.

CHAPTER 16

T he moment Werner entered the lecture hall where the student board met, he felt a wave of hostility directed toward him. Looking into the discontented faces of the members he realized the mood was about to boil over.

It didn't come as a surprise, because he'd observed the growing dissatisfaction for several weeks now and sensed the students were up to something. He just hadn't expected the revolt to come so soon. After the glorious inauguration students had expected a bed of roses. But with the promotion of communist propaganda being disseminated throughout the departments, rumblings among them had increased daily.

Werner had discussed this issue with Norbert, but as always, the answer had been rehashed lines of party wisdom, rather than substantial advice he could use in practice.

He sighed, some days he felt so disheartened. Deceived even. His aspirations for a democratic socialist rule in Germany, as touted by Stalin and his followers, had turned out to be nothing but illusions. *Communism has let you down.* He quickly shook his head. Traitorous thoughts like this transported a person to a gulag faster than he could blink.

"Quiet, please," he called out as he took his place at the professor's podium. His gaze wandered across the members of the student board. It consisted of one dozen communist hardliners and another dozen carefully screened men and women from other parties. Three each were Social Democrats and Christian Democrats, one girl belonged to the Liberal Democrats and the rest had no party affiliation, but all of them were considered fervent anti-fascists. None of them had ever belonged to the NSDAP, and some, like Georg, had even been victimized at the hands of the Nazis.

A part of him could understand their plight, but of course he couldn't let them know this. Norbert had been clear in his instructions to nip the threatening revolt in the bud. The noise ebbed away and he said, "May the chairman of the student board please speak up?"

Georg stood, his brown hair tousled from desperately running his hand through it. It was a gesture Werner had observed in the other man many times, when he disliked a situation. "We are here to officially protest flying the Soviet flag atop our university. We're not a Soviet institution."

Werner sighed with relief. This would be a lot easier to appease than he'd feared. "This is only temporary. The flag was raised to celebrate the upcoming first anniversary of the liberation of Berlin. All of you should be grateful for the great sacrifices of the Red Army to return freedom to their German brothers."

Looking into the faces of the students, he realized that his argument wasn't having the intended effect. He needed to present a different angle. "In fact, everyone in this room should be proud," he let his eyes rest on each of them before he continued, "for your contribution in bringing down Hitler's fascist regime."

Several of the communist students clapped their hands as if on cue. Werner suppressed a smile. "But seeing that your own efforts haven't been sufficiently appreciated, I'll suggest to General Sokolov flying the German flag beside the Soviet one in united friendship."

There was a low murmur in the lecture hall, but nobody dared to openly oppose his peace offering.

Georg raised his voice again. "We also protest the political indoctrination in all fields of study."

This accusation was much more difficult to counter, and Werner thought for a moment. Georg was a bright young man and would easily see through the usual distortion of facts used by the propaganda department.

He decided to revert to a proven tactic and said, "There must be some misunderstanding. The Soviet Commandant personally has endorsed the reopening of Berlin University with great personal, material and financial effort. The best professors have been chosen to teach the fields of natural sciences, philosophy, medicine, veterinary, agriculture, law and theology."

He paused for effect and once again met the eyes of each individual in the room. "You are the brightest men and women of your generation, destined to continue the fight against fascism and the..." He caught himself before saying *imperial West* and opted to omit the dig against the class enemy. "... plutocracy. United we stand strong and can overcome a dozen years of the unlawful Nazi regime. This is the very reason why the Soviet Union, and we, the new democratic Berlin administration, place such great emphasis upon education."

But Georg didn't relent. "There is no misunderstanding, Herr Böhm. We are displeased at the amount of propaganda promoted at this university. We are students of our relative disciplines, none of us signed up for politics. The Soviet misinformation has permeated our subjects and become part and parcel of the arts and sciences we study. In this way, incorrect data is included in subjects and distorts the truths of our topics. It is also noticed that any printed material that is considered undesirable is being redacted and eliminated, and replaced with communist dogma to ensure that the Soviet ideological spin is put on every published item."

Werner had the strongest foreboding that Georg wouldn't end well. Too eager was the young man to stand up for his beliefs and defend the newly acquired liberties of the German students. But he shoved the nasty feeling aside and concentrated on the task at hand.

Right now, it was of paramount importance that he quieten the rising discontent before it became uncontainable. From his own experience he knew that the decision makers in Moscow weren't squeamish in their treatment of perceived dissenters. Couldn't these students understand that for their own sakes it was best to keep their mouths shut?

"I trust you have evidence to back up your accusations," Werner asked, and Georg held up a fat file in response.

"Rest assured, we have discussed these unnecessary inclusions thoroughly, and demand an immediate stop to this insidious, destructive scheme to turn us into a generation of communists. We students are questioning whether the Soviets really want a democratic Germany."

"Yes, of course this is what we want for Germany. Surely our praise for our system is being misconstrued," argued Werner, desperate to defuse the current of discontent. "We are all going through a transitional phase. This university is a prime example of the Soviet initiative to rebuild your nation.

Quality, free education is being imparted here. Where else will you find such commitment and generosity?"

Since his arrival in Berlin almost a year earlier, so many things had happened and bit by bit had chipped away at his belief in Stalin's infallibility, but that didn't mean that Werner had stopped believing in the superiority of the socialist way. Once the transition period was over, everyone would accept that socialism was the only system giving its citizens liberty, wealth and participation and was certainly preferable to living under a totalitarian capitalist regime.

"Incidentally, the Americans are offering to sponsor a university in their sector," a spunky redhead called Lotte Klausen said.

Werner perked up his ears. It was the first time he had heard of plans for such a bold transgression of the quadripartite agreement. He made a mental note to inform Norbert about the newest American atrocity, before he fixed his gaze on the young woman. "I would advise the exercise of extreme caution when dealing with Americans. Their country is a bastion of imperial oppression, an evil and corrupt reigning class in the death throes of capitalism."

"More Soviet propaganda!" a tall, skinny man with blond curly hair shouted from the back. Werner recognized him as Julian Berger, a student of chemistry.

He raised his hand to stop the hecklers, all dying to voice their viewpoints. It was time to stop the charade. Any further deviation from the dictates of the official doctrine would merit a trial, and if he couldn't contain the subversive remarks within this room, there'd soon be blood on the walls.

"I will certainly look into the matter and consult the Board of Directors who will, I'm sure, investigate and put a stop to any issues that distract from the peace and good intentions of the institution. This meeting is over. Thank you for your time and interest," Werner said in a tone that left no doubt this was his last word on the matter.

Almost by a miracle the students left the lecture hall, peacefully, yet grumbling. But this was a problem for another day. First, he had to alert Norbert about the American plan to open up their own university.

CHAPTER 17

Marlene adapted to the grueling daily routine of working at the hospital, queuing up for rations, and running errands on top of attending classes and studying at home. In the first weeks, she'd fallen to bed exhausted every night, but slowly her body seemed to overcome the need for sleep and she could do mostly with a few hours a night. To everyone concerned about her health, she jokingly said that she could sleep all she wanted once she was dead.

The main reason why she jumped out of her bed every morning with unmatched energy was the prospect of seeing Werner. She still didn't admit to anyone – even herself – that she had feelings for him, but simply the hope of catching a fleeting glance of him in the university hallways made her entire body shiver with anticipation.

He seemed equally eager to see her, because he often happened to walk past the doors of her lecture hall at the precise moment when her class ended. Usually he wouldn't say a word, but his charming smile always warmed her heart, despite knowing that it was wrong to fancy a convinced communist like him.

She'd been more or less indifferent to the Nazi propaganda at the beginning but had come to hate the oppression, brutality, distortion of facts and, most of all, the crippling hatred for anyone who was different, as the years passed.

Now she saw the Soviets for what they really were. They hadn't come as the liberators they liked to call themselves, but as oppressors, and their ultimate goal was to install another totalitarian regime in Germany. She never believed the honeyed words of General Sokolov and his cronies who said one thing and then did another one.

One day she left the civil law lecture together with her fellow student Lotte, a quick-witted redhead with a sharp tongue. The two of them had quickly become friends and spent plenty of time together to study and compare notes. Other students often commented that a pair of girls couldn't be more different than the two of them.

Lotte was impulsive, driven, outspoken and assertive, where Marlene was composed, cautious, careful and kind. They even studied law for different reasons. Marlene wanted to help people, while Lotte wanted to fight for justice. But despite their differences they hit it off right away. Marlene liked the other girl for her inner strength to stand up for herself, but she also felt the need to care for her, because she often looked so sad.

"I gotta run, my sister is waiting for me. See you in the morning?" Lotte said and turned on her heel to rush off.

Nostalgia wound its way into Marlene's heart. Both of her brothers were still in captivity. Kurt was somewhere in France and Albert had been shipped to America. Her eyes to the ground she walked down the hallway, suddenly feeling lost, when she all but bumped into another person.

"I'm sorry," she mumbled. Looking up she stared into Herr Böhm's face and straightened her back. "Herr Böhm, please excuse me, I wasn't paying attention."

"Nothing to worry about. This is a pleasant surprise, actually." He rubbed his clean-shaven chin, looking more like an insecure boy than one of the leading men in Berlin.

Marlene stood frozen in place. She didn't move and they must have stood like this for an entire minute, while other students passed by until the lecture hall had emptied and they stood alone in the hallway.

Towering over her by almost one foot, he said, "Why don't we have a cup of coffee in my office instead of standing in this drafty corridor, Fräulein Kupfer, since I'd like to make a proposal to you."

A proposal? Her head whirled and she barely managed to nod. Her feet automatically falling in step with him, she scolded herself for having completely inappropriate thoughts. He'd never even touched her apart from the formal kiss on her hand. How on earth could she dream about a white dress? She almost laughed out loud at the hilarity of her train of thought.

His secretary Frau Busch cast a questioning look at Marlene but didn't say a word. She probably realized that keeping her job meant never questioning her boss's moves.

"Bring us two cups of coffee, please," Herr Böhm said without further explanation and held his office door open for Marlene. He motioned for her to sit in front of his desk. The only other time she'd been in his office was during her admission interview, but then a guard and Professor Klein had been present as well. Being alone with Herr Böhm in the same room unnerved her.

He walked over to one of the bookshelves overflowing with four-ring binders, folders and all kinds of books, and she wondered what exactly he wanted from her. The tension raised her neck hair, and while listening with one ear to the noises Frau Busch made brewing coffee, Marlene scrutinized his office.

It was by far the nicest room in the entire building. Fresh white paint adorned the dilapidated walls and covered up the damaged plaster. The huge oak desk prominently stood in the middle of the room with a throne-like armchair for Böhm. She had heard of the intimidating experience of his staring down on the visitor who sat on a much smaller metal chair in front of the desk. Suddenly she felt small and vulnerable.

He walked over with a book in his hands at the same time as Frau Busch entered the office with two cups of coffee – real coffee – on a tray.

"Thank you, Frau Busch, you may leave for today," Böhm dismissed his secretary without further explanation. When she closed the door, Böhm handed Marlene one cup and instead of retreating behind his monumental desk to stare down on her, he leaned against it and smiled. "Do you take sugar?"

"Sugar?" Marlene shrugged. What kind of question was this? Where she was concerned, sugar had long ago ceased to exist.

"In your coffee?" His lips tipped into a smile and Marlene observed with amazement how the color of his eyes changed from a cold gray to a most inviting warm green.

"Yes, please."

He took the cup from her, added a spoonful of sugar, stirred it and handed it back to her. "Now, please taste."

She took a sip, her brain not quite comprehending what was happening, except for the fuzzy warm feeling spreading through her body. Her taste buds exploded with the bitter-sweet aroma filling her mouth and she all but moaned, "Delicious." How wonderful it would be to take such luxuries for granted as she once did all those many years ago.

His smile increased, as did the butterflies in her stomach. Marlene couldn't help thinking that maybe Bruni was right and encouraging the handsome, well-groomed, charming, intelligent, and likeable man wasn't a bad thing. Why did she want to miss out on the way he made her feel, just because she hated the Soviets? What did politics have to do with feelings?

"I've been wanting to give you this book," Böhm suddenly said with his deep well-modulated voice. "It was one of my favorites at grammar school."

Marlene looked at a worn-out copy of Anna Segher's novel *Aufstand der Fischer von Santa Barbara,* Revolt of the Fishermen of Santa Barbara, and gasped. She remembered all too well the event when students of the same university she attended now had burned thousands of books banned by the Nazis, Anna Segher's novel one of them.

"There's nothing to be afraid of. Hitler is gone and with him the time of tyranny and fear. Please, I want you to read it. It will help you understand how the revolution of the working class will finally lead to prosperity and happiness for all." He pressed the book into her hands.

"I...I don't know what to say. Thank you so much, Herr Böhm," she stammered. The book must have been dear to him and giving it to her was such a thoughtful, generous gesture. She was moved beyond words. Whoever said that Böhm – or Werner, as she secretly called him – was cold-hearted and cruel certainly hadn't taken the time to look behind his façade.

"May I call you Marlene, please?" His voice was soft and throaty, as if caressing her.

She nodded, surprised. "Certainly."

"And please call me Werner, will you?"

Her eyes widened. It wouldn't be appropriate at all to call a member of the Berlin administration by their first name. The only persons at the university who did this were the communist members of the student board, and Georg. Her dear friend and Böhm – Werner – had become fast friends and Georg had been propelled into a prominent position thanks to his mentor.

"You don't have to, if it causes you chagrin," Werner said.

"No, no. I'd love to, but wouldn't it be inappropriate to do so here at the university? I mean, I'm just a student and you're…"

He gave a chuckle that reverberated through her bones. "Not at all. Your worries are founded in the traditional class system, but under the socialist ideology all people are equal and there's no need to distinguish social rank by using last names." Seeing that she was still wavering, he said, "But if it makes you feel more comfortable, you can still address me as Herr Böhm when we're in public."

Her heart stopped beating. His answer implied that he envisioned meetings in the future with only the two of them present.

He looked at her, happy and sad at the same time, before he raised his voice again. "I'm worried about your friend Georg."

Her eyes snapped wide open. That man certainly had a talent for ruining a romantic moment. "About Georg?" The stupid question was out of her mouth before it dawned on her. He must be jealous of the other man. He might even assume Georg and Marlene were walking together. "No…there's no reason…I mean he and I are just friends."

Werner put a warm hand on hers, but the concern in his eyes increased. "That's not what I'm talking about. I'm worried about his safety."

"His safety?" Marlene felt like a retard, too slow to understand the world around her. What had Werner to do with Georg's safety? And why should he be worried?

"See," he sighed, obviously uncomfortable with the topic.

"It's just, he's been voicing his criticism about the Soviets so adamantly, people have noticed. Powerful people." His eyes bored into hers, willing her to understand. "While suggestions for improvement are welcome and necessary, constant nagging isn't. I personally believe he's doing this with the best intentions, but others are not so benevolent in their judgment. There's even the suspicion that he's been hired by enemies of the people to undermine the successful functioning of the university and thus deny education to the German people."

Marlene's jaw dropped to the floor and she sprang up. "No, no, Georg would never...he's the most honest, upright and incorruptible person I know. Did you know that the Nazis sent him to Mauthausen, because he criticized them?"

"I certainly do." Of course he did. It was said the Soviets had a file on every person in Berlin. "And as I said, I have nothing but the highest opinion of Georg. But he needs to tread carefully and avoid further annoying our Soviet benefactors." She didn't think the Russians were benefactors. "Will you please tell him to tone down his opposition, at least for a while? Until things have calmed down?"

She squinted her eyes at Werner and a terrible suspicion stabbed deep into her heart. Her eyes blazing with anger, she spit out the words. "So, the coffee, the book, the first name, all of this was a ruse to get me to help you deal with a critic of your glorious communist ideology?"

"No..." He looked at her with so much hurt, she almost doubled over. But this couldn't deter her from giving him the cold shoulder.

"I should leave. I have homework to do. Good night, Herr Böhm," she said with the iciest tone she could muster and quickly left the office, her head raised high. Only when she'd left the long hallways behind and stepped out on the street did she notice she was still carrying his book. *Damn him*!

CHAPTER 18

Werner was flummoxed. He might have a way with words, but understanding a woman was way beyond his capabilities. Shaking his head, he returned to his desk, wondering what he'd done wrong. Shouldn't Marlene be pleased that he was looking out for her friend?

The ringing telephone interrupted his thoughts and he answered it, "Werner Böhm."

"Hey, Werner, it's Norbert. You haven't forgotten the party invitation from the Americans, have you?"

Shoot. "Of course not." Werner glanced at his wristwatch. The party had already started. "I called at your office," he lied, "that I'm running late, but I'm on my way as we speak."

"Hurry up, you're missing out," Norbert laughed and hung up.

Nothing was further from his mind than chatting and drinking with rowdy men he'd never seen before. But in post-war Berlin invitations and return invitations by the four victorious powers came hard and fast. While the Germans suffered from food shortages, the Allies certainly were intent on bathing the city in vodka, champagne, beer or tea, according to their national preferences.

Norbert was already in a discussion with several Western officers at the time Werner arrived, one of them Dean Harris, the American Commandant in Berlin. Werner quite liked the man, because he was intelligent, listened intently and had a sensible, laid-back attitude. Werner suspected that beneath the cool surface lay a hot temper, but he'd never once seen Harris explode in public, unlike General Sokolov, who was famous for chewing out the asses of his own men and deluging the Western members of the Kommandatura with obloquy.

Sokolov especially disliked Harris and had given him several unflattering nicknames he liked to use in press releases and on radio, among them Brute Colonel, Enemy of Democracy and Beast of Berlin – his current favorite.

Werner usually cringed at the general's unstatesmanlike behavior and often wondered what Harris thought about the insults. Did he even take his Russian counterpart seriously when Sokolov used name-calling like a toddler throwing a temper tantrum?

For obvious reasons he never once voiced his concerns, or his secret admiration for the American colonel who always took the abuse in his stride.

Norbert had noticed him and waved him over. "There you are."

"Comrade Norbert, Kommandant Harris, I must excuse my late arrival, I had business to attend to at the university," Werner said.

"No worries, this is a party, not a work meeting," Harris replied and waved at a waitress to bring Werner a beer. The group engaged in harmless small talk, and he relished the opportunity to practice his English language skills.

Back in Moscow he had studied at the Institute for Foreign

Languages in the department of English. In the beginning of the occupation he'd been told to listen in on the conversations of the Americans without speaking himself, but they'd soon discovered his mastery of their language and guarded their tongues when he was nearby. Which was a situation he actually favored, because the deceptive work of a spy for the Soviet High Command wasn't something he enjoyed.

After some time, Captain Orlovski walked up to Werner and said, "Can I talk to you for a minute?"

"Will you excuse me please," Werner said to Harris and turned to leave with Orlovski. Despite sincerely enjoying the company of Harris, a wave of relief flooded his body. It was never good to appear too friendly with a foreigner, even though they were supposedly allies.

"I take it you have heard about the upcoming city council elections?" Orlovski asked.

"Naturally." Werner nodded. Sokolov had done his best to resist the foolish idea of free elections at such an early point in time, since it was a known fact that the German people were not yet ready for self-government and too much freedom would only lead to disaster. But in the end, he'd had to succumb to the insistent nagging of the Western Allies, spear-headed by Colonel Harris.

"I'm in charge of the logistics, and Sokolov suggested I enlist your help with agitation and propaganda."

A suggestion by Sokolov was actually an order that Werner couldn't refuse. "Certainly, whatever you need."

"Let's get together in my office tomorrow around noon and discuss the tasks," Orlovski said, before he bid his goodbyes.

Werner gazed after him for a long time. Both of them knew it was essential to win the elections. Otherwise the communists would lose their stronghold over Berlin and possibly over all of Germany.

Their carefully installed control was slowly slipping away, especially after the stubborn Social Democrats had refused to join the newly founded SED, the Socialist Unity Party. Werner himself was dealing with the consequences of this brazen attempt to splinter the unity of the working people.

He cursed the involvement of well-known Social Democrats like Kurt Schumacher, who had visited Berlin to agitate against the best interests of his compatriots. Without them, the unification of the KPD and SPD would have passed off without a hitch. And without this precedent of rebellion the university students wouldn't have dared to present their audacious demands for academic freedom.

He came to the conclusion that helping Orlovski influence the elections in favor of the communists was actually time well spent, because it would at the same time solve Werner's own problems with the dissenting students.

The next day Norbert relieved him of his duties at the university and Werner fully immersed himself in preparations for the elections. Usually, he arrived at his new office at the Haus der Einheit, the house of unity, well before everyone else and stayed long into the night.

Despite working fifteen to sixteen hours a day, he missed seeing Marlene, missed her bright smile and the excitement in her eyes when she looked at him. But that was a thing of the past, because on the rare occasions when their paths crossed, she turned her head away. It stabbed at his heart and he threw himself even deeper into work.

The eyes of the entire world rested upon Berlin, because for the first time in more than a dozen years there would be free elections in the city. Sokolov had many times emphasized that these elections would decide the political landscape in Europe for decades to come. A landslide victory of the SED was expected, and Feodor Orlovski and Werner both knew their own fates were intrinsically connected with these elections.

Werner wouldn't take any chances on the outcome and devised a plan that included generously doling out pens and notebooks to schoolchildren, soup kitchens for workers, and augmented food and coal rations – for Berliners living in the Soviet sector.

Money was not an issue, as he'd been given a free hand to use any and all resources of the Soviet-occupied zone in Germany. Werner secured dozens of volunteers to canvass for the SED and diverted food transports destined for Dresden, Leipzig, Chemnitz, Jena or Magdeburg to the capital. He equipped the SED with as much paper, pens, paint, and cloth for posters, pamphlets and banners as needed, while at the same time denying these resources to the other political parties.

Every single one of the benevolent actions came with a clear message about where the goods came from and how much more pleasant a life under communist rule would be than under the imperialist oppression.

But as time passed, it became clear that the strategy of dangling carrots would not prove sufficient. At one of their strategy meetings, a member of the polling committee said, "Comrade Böhm, I'm afraid the Berliners don't know what is good for them. Despite all our efforts, the polls seem to favor the other parties over the SED."

Werner all but doubled over by this punch in the pit of the stomach. He was out of ideas.

"We have to make sure the SED comes out on top," Orlovski blurted out desperately. "There will be dire consequences unless this happens. I'm sure you know what I mean. Our current prospects are not acceptable."

Silence fell over the room, because everyone knew what

Orlovski was talking about. Werner had an unwelcome flash-back to the time of the purges in the Soviet Union – the time when one by one, his parents, his teachers, his neighbors, and even his classmates had been arrested by the NKVD and vanished into oblivion.

Normally he buried thoughts of his parents deep down in his heart, too painful were the memories. And it was too much shame he felt when thinking of how they must have suffered in some Siberian camp while he was enjoying his life. For a long time, he'd grappled with the injustice of their arrest. They were innocent, he knew. His sweet, caring mother had never been a vicious spy, abominable traitor to the Soviet people and doggish agitator for the imperialist West. Neither had his stern but correct father.

But his personal fate hadn't deterred his belief about the greater good. Certainly, the NKVD knew more than he did, or perhaps some innocents inevitably got caught in the net together with the actual criminals. He shrugged. Going down that lane was a futile waste of time.

Into the uncomfortable silence, a member of the loyal communist-installed Markgraf police took the floor. "Com-rades, if I may suggest something."

"Go ahead, Comrade Dante," Werner encouraged the young policeman. He'd never thought the man one of the bright sort, more the bully, pushing others around, but if he had an idea Werner wanted to hear about it.

"Since showing the voters all the good our party offers them doesn't work, maybe we should try it the other way round and let them experience what exactly dissenters can expect."

"My department can't condone the use of violence." Werner did not want to hear any more suggestions.

But Orlovski gave him a cold stare. "My orders are to win

us this election at any cost, and your task is to help me, just like I helped you with the university."

Hot shudders ran down Werner's spine. Orlovski was collecting the favor, and there was nothing Werner could do to extricate himself from this nasty situation. He bowed his head to show his acceptance.

Orlovski encouraged the other man. "We certainly need more drastic measures, so what do you suggest?"

Dante rose to his full height of close to six feet and a smug smile appeared on his round face beneath a bald head. "We can easily organize squads to break up meetings of opposing parties, obstruct whatever activities they plan and give a good beating to those who don't succumb to our threats."

Werner shook his head. "We have agreed to free elections. The Americans will cry wolf if they find out."

"Let them cry," Orlovski said. "If the electorate isn't amenable to words, they must find out that their traitorous behavior has consequences. I say, give the Markgraf police a free hand."

Dante gave a vile grin and wrung his hands in giddy antici-pation. "We can pay some of the candidates a social call and see if they still want to be nominated for election."

"Isn't that a bit extreme?" a young woman in charge of the soup kitchens asked.

"Yes, it is," Orlovski growled at her. "But extreme situations require extreme measures. We need to alter the composition of the electorate. Disenfranchise everyone known to be a dissenter. Attack polling stations in primarily imperialist areas, hinder people from turning up to cast their vote. Kidnap key candidates, threaten them and their families to keep them out of the race. If the only way to beat the cheating and lying Western Imperialists is to rig the election in any way we can, then we must do it. It is our patriotic duty to secure a victory for the SED."

Frenetic applause surged through the room. Werner kept quiet. He couldn't condone such a heinous strategy, but neither could he refuse. Glancing at the men present he recognized deep-rooted fanaticism in the eyes of each one of them, apart from the young woman who'd spoken up earlier.

The renewed enthusiasm about the new direction their campaign was taking was palpable in the room. He had never felt more ashamed of his comrades – and of himself – than at this very moment.

"Well then, it's decided. Everything is allowed, as long as it ensures our victory. Go out and do your work," Orlovski said, concluding the meeting.

CHAPTER 19

As much as Marlene avoided Werner, she secretly longed to see him. But since the Kommandatura had announced the elections to the City Council this coming October 20th, he rarely showed up at the university.

The times she saw him, she quickly looked away and pretended not to notice, despite having waited for this one glimpse for days. Her emotions were infuriating. Despite her best intentions she'd started reading Anna Segher's novel, especially after she'd found comments in his handwriting on the pages.

His remarks were so thoughtful and showed so much concern for the general wellbeing of the people, she found it difficult to reconcile them with the calculating behavior he practiced these days.

In spite of his pleas, she had not relayed his warning to Georg, since she refused to become a stooge for the communist cause. And nothing had happened either, which only proved her point. In fact, due to the upcoming elections, the student board members had diverted their focus to helping their preferred parties, in the certainty that with a new city council other things would change too.

Almost without noticing, summer break had sneaked up on them and Lotte said, "It's kind of sad not to come here for the next weeks."

Marlene laughed. "What's sad about not having to work, attend classes and study twenty-four hours a day plus running errands and doing chores in the night?"

Lotte joined her laughter. "You're right. Working only one job will be a reprieve, but I will miss seeing my friends."

"Why can't you see your friends?" Marlene asked, slightly confused. "Are you traveling?"

"As if anyone could travel these days." Lotte moved her head the same way Marlene always did when she threw her hair behind her shoulder. It was a peculiar and forlorn gesture, since Lotte wore her hair almost as short as a man's.

"Why did you cut your hair?" Marlene asked without thinking.

"Because..." The happy laughter fell from Lotte's face. "...it was the right thing to do." Her curt answer clearly indicated that she wouldn't discuss this topic any further and Marlene wondered what lay beneath the funny, witty, tough, impulsive and caring surface of her friend.

Lotte rarely, if ever, talked about her past and the only thing Marlene knew was that she'd spent some time in a concentration camp. Her entire body shivered at the thought. Two of her new friends, Lotte and Georg, had been camp inmates during Hitler's reign, while she had never given a single thought to what really happened inside the barbed wire fence.

She'd unquestioningly believed the story told by her parents, teachers and the press, that those were prisons to re-educate the workshy, homosexuals, asocials and other elements that posed a danger to the German people.

Now that the truth had been unearthed, all the little signs here and there made sense. The skeletal people in striped prison garb cleaning the rubble after each air raid, the hollow eyes begging for food, the…

"Hey? Are you okay?" Lotte asked, grabbing her arm. "You're suddenly white as a sheet."

Marlene shook her head to disperse the troubling images. "I'm fine, really."

"You sure you don't want to sit down?"

"Yes. Let's go outside, I probably am just overtired," she lied. Because, what should she tell her friend? That she felt guilty and ashamed for not having noticed? For not having paid attention? And if she had…what would she have done? Looked away like everyone else? Another icy shiver ran down her spine and filled her legs with jelly.

With her last ounce of strength, she pulled herself together and followed Lotte outside into the sunshine.

In front of the university, hundreds of workers, mostly women, were busy clearing rubble from a ruin. They formed a long chain from the top of the rubble mountain all the way down to the street, where a truck was parked, eager to gobble up all the demolition waste.

"How amazing it's going to be when all the destruction is cleared and we have buildings and streets again," Lotte said as Marlene pictured the scene.

"It'll be many years before this happens," she said, wearily. "Some days I can't envision any more how a real city with real buildings looks like."

"You certainly need a break." The short moment of gloom had passed, and Lotte was as upbeat as usual. "Let's go somewhere nice."

"Somewhere nice? Like where?" Marlene suddenly felt the burden of the entire world resting on her shoulders, wondering whether she could ever feel happy again. It was very much unlike her, and she began to worry that something was messing with her head.

"Yes. Let's go to the lake." Lotte jumped up as if she was sitting on a swarm of bumblebees. "I know a place where we can swim."

"Swim? But...I don't have a bathing suit."

"You don't need one, we'll stay in our knickers," Lotte giggled.

The suggestion was so outrageous Marlene felt herself blushing furiously. But Lotte seemed not to notice and insisted, "Let's go."

"Right now?"

"Yes, right now. Wasn't this our last day of school and don't we have the entire afternoon off? And isn't the sun shining like crazy, personally urging us to go have a swim?" Lotte wouldn't be deterred. Once this girl had made up her mind, she was harder to derail than a tank moving at full speed.

They took the bus to the huge Wannsee lake and just like Lotte had promised, they found a secluded spot devoid of any other people. Lotte stripped down to her knickers and camisole and jumped right into the water, but Marlene couldn't bring herself to do the same. She took off only her shoes and socks, gathered her skirt and cooled down her legs up to the knees in the refreshing water.

Later, they lazed in the sun, doing absolutely nothing at all for the first time in months. Exhausted from months of sleep deprivation, Marlene dozed off until she felt Lotte's arm on her shoulder. "Hey, sleepyhead, we need to return home."

"Have I slept the entire afternoon?" Marlene asked, stupefied.

"Yes, you did. But don't worry. I read a book during that time." Lotte showed her a worn-out book with a plain brown protective cover and the label that identified it as a university library book.

"You've been reading a law book?" Marlene propped herself up on her elbows, giving her friend an incredulous look.

"Of course not," Lotte giggled. "I'm not that ambitious. I found it in the German literature section, it's called *Aufstand der Fischer von Santa Barbara* by …"

"Anna Segher," Marlene completed her sentence.

"How do you know? Have you read it?"

"Yes. It's really good. Werner Böhm gave it to me." The words had stumbled out of her mouth before she even thought about it.

"Herr Böhm? Seriously?" Lotte pursed her lips.

Marlene felt the blood rushing to her cheeks and cursed her habit of flushing so easily. It didn't matter what she said next, or whether she said anything at all, since Lotte for sure had already drawn her own conclusions.

"So, what's with you and him?" Lotte asked.

"Nothing. Absolutely nothing," came the sharp reply.

"Uh-uh, I know infatuation when I see it. And he's clearly smitten by you, in case you haven't noticed." Lotte stated the obvious.

"That's his problem, not mine," Marlene insisted while her friend laughed, not willing to let go of the topic yet.

"So, the dreamy gaze in your eyes every time he passes by doesn't mean anything?"

"No, it doesn't."

"But why? He seems nice enough, besides being so handsome," Lotte probed. "What gives?"

"I'm not into communists," Marlene explained. "We have suffered enough with one dictatorial regime, we don't need more of the same. If the Russians have their way it will be back to terror all around. Have you heard about the vicious things they do to our prisoners of war?"

"I know all too well, my boyfriend is one of them," Lotte said with the saddest expression Marlene had ever seen on her face.

She wrapped her arms around her friend and murmured, "I'm so sorry, Lotte. But you'll see, he'll soon come home. The war's been over for more than a year and the Allies are releasing more prisoners every day."

CHAPTER 20

Dean was in his office with his deputy Jason Gardner and glaring in disbelief at the report in front of them. The Russians had set the wheels of villainy in motion and the bribes, tricks, threats and other shenanigans they used to rig the elections in their favor made every other crooked politician the world had seen look like a monk.

He'd patiently weathered the spiteful abuse the Soviets had showered on him personally and the Western Allies in general every single day since the decision to hold city council elections, but their latest disinformation campaign, filled with lies, phony promises and intimidation was simply too much.

"Jason, we need to have our own voice," Dean said.

"You know, the Russians won't give us airtime on Radio Berlin," Jason said.

Dean knew that his deputy had run from pillar to post in his efforts to convince the Russians to put Radio Berlin under quadripartite administration or at least give the other powers airtime.

The Soviet Military Administration hedged, stalled, and

prevaricated until they outright refused, which was even more annoying, because the *Haus des Rundfunks*, the radio headquarters, was located in the Masurenallee, deep in the British sector, while the transmitters stood in Tegel, in the French sector. And still the miserable Russian hoodlums claimed the radio station for themselves and controlled access to airtime.

He slammed his fist on the desk. "I'm not taking their shit any longer. I want my own radio station."

Jason looked up in stunned surprise, but quickly composed himself again. "It's not that easy. You know that we don't have a broadcasting tower and can only distribute our *Drahtfunk in the American Sector* program by telephone line."

"I don't care. Get me Captain Barley right now."

Twenty minutes later Jason returned with the Army engineer, whose fame for being a gifted inventor, fiddler and often a savior in cases of need preceded him. He was smallish and thin, gaunt even, and his graying hair sometimes deluded people into underestimating him, but given as much as a piece of wire he could fix basically any technical problem.

"Colonel Harris, you wanted to see me?" Captain Barley greeted Dean.

"Yes, Captain. I need a broadcasting tower."

Barley's eyes widened and he apparently didn't know what to reply to such an unusual request. "I'm sorry, sir. I'm not sure I understand correctly."

"Let me put it this way: The Soviets are making my life miserable spewing their spiteful propaganda over Radio Berlin. What is worse, the democratic parties are in danger of losing the elections if we cannot provide the German people with objective facts countering the Russian lies and intimidation. Therefore, I want my own radio station."

"By when do you need to go on air?" Captain Barley asked.

Dean almost let out a chuckle. That's what he liked about

the engineer. He never said it was impossible, but instead accepted the challenge. "Well before the elections."

Election day was a mere seven weeks away and by all normal standards what Dean was asking was simply impossible. Barley rubbed his chin, deep in thought, and didn't answer for a long while.

"A broadcasting tower is impossible on such short notice," he finally said. "But I have another idea. It's not ideal, because the power is only eight hundred watts, but you can have it by the end of the week."

Dean all but jumped up from his seat, giddy to know more about the wonder apparatus Barley was offering. "Sounds like a plan. What are you thinking about?"

Now Barley was in his element and explained about mobile units with a terrestrial mid-wave transmitter, a wire stretched between two wooden poles for an antenna, and a myriad of other technical details Dean didn't have the patience to listen to.

"Prioritize this task over anything else and report back to me the moment you're done," he interrupted the engineer, who was positively glowing with enthusiasm.

When Barley had left the room Dean said, "Jason, tell the DIAS staff that they're about to go on air."

"Shouldn't we think of a new name, too?" Jason asked. "*Drahtfunk* doesn't describe it, since we won't be transmitting over phone wires anymore."

"You're right. Tell everyone we have a new sender, Radio in the American Sector, short RIAS Berlin."

By the end of the week Captain Barley returned and asked Dean to accompany him for a test drive of the new transmitter. And on September 4 Dean personally opened the first program with the words, "Here is RIAS Berlin, radio in the American sector. You hear us on medium wave 611 kHz." And he ended his short speech with the words, "RIAS Berlin – a free voice in a free world!"

Operation Backtalk had started and now RIAS Berlin broadcasted every day, debunking the lies and myths the Russians spewed, but Dean still couldn't be sure the Russians wouldn't get their way. Thus, he made one last effort to keep the Russians from stealing the first free elections in Berlin and put the point of mutual supervision of the polling stations on election day on the agenda.

General Sokolov was not amused and spun a long speech about the virtues of democracy and how the Americans tried to subdue the working people.

"I'm sick and tired of your prevarication. Not a single issue in the Kommandatura can be agreed upon without lengthy, unnecessary and outright stupid discussions," Dean accused General Sokolov.

"Nothing's perfect but Comrade Stalin is highly supportive of the first free and fair democratic election process for the people of Berlin. Only thanks to our liberation—"

"If your Comrade Stalin is so fond of free elections, then you'll have no problem with quadripartite oversight," Dean cut the general short. "Or would you rather go against Stalin's wishes?"

Sokolov gritted his teeth and agreed, while Dean felt a surge of elation course through his veins. It was not often that he could wrangle even the tiniest concession from the general.

It was a small victory, albeit an important one.

On election day military jeeps with representatives from each of the four Allied powers patrolled Berlin, making regular rounds of the polling stations to see that no irregularities occurred.

Dean was in a jeep with Captain Orlovski, Major Bouchard and General Wilson. All of Berlin was on its feet going to the polling stations and the voter turnout exceeded Dean's wildest expectations.

It seemed the citizens understood that the result of the vote would have profound implications for their future. Though tensions across the city had been steadily building, people arrived early and queued patiently for their turn to cast their ballot. Sometimes a scuffle broke out, but unarmed German police quickly solved the issues, and if not, they called the Allied military police to take care of extraordinarily stubborn troublemakers. All in all, it was a peaceful affair.

Suddenly, a group of boisterous campaigners blocked the road as they walked across, shouting slogans and waving their party flags in front of the jeep.

"Look at them!" Orlovski remarked. "It's the same everywhere in this city. Happy people who are delighted with this move toward progress. This is true democracy."

Dean shot a look at the Russian, who'd been, together with Werner Böhm, the mastermind behind the deliberate disinformation campaign and the more sinister events that had happened during the lead-up to this day.

"Two leading Social Democrats were abducted a week ago by the Markgraf police," Dean said in a cold voice. "This is not an isolated incident, as other party members have been paid a visit by your thugs and were only released when they resigned from their posts."

"The Soviet Military Administration cannot be made responsible for the vicious acts of individual members of the German police," Orlovski said, despite the fact that everyone in Berlin knew quite well that the chief of police, Paul Markgraf, was a Soviet puppet. "Do you have any indication of the culprits' identities?"

"Yes, we do have information on the perpetrators and are following up our leads," Dean replied guardedly.

"Withholding such information from the SMAD is against the Yalta agreement of quadripartite rule," Orlovski snapped.

Dean had the greatest desire to laugh out loud. Orlovski could not actually believe the bullshit he was spouting. The Soviets withheld information from their allies on a daily basis.

"We'll let you know the results of our surveillance," Dean said with a smug grin. "Who knows what trash we'll discover in our dragnet?"

Orlovski shrugged haughtily, not deigning to reply.

"I hope that after the elections, the communists will give up their stranglehold on Berlin and accept the will of the people," Harris said quietly to Wilson. "I'm fed up with their antics."

"We can only hope, old chap, but I fear they are never going to relinquish their power if they can help it," Wilson replied.

At eight p.m. the polling stations closed and the tedious task of getting the paper ballots to the city hall and counting them began. Time progressed and the ballot boxes from Köpenick, a stronghold of the social democrats, still hadn't arrived.

"What's wrong?" Dean asked one of the members of the organizing committee.

The German man stepped uncomfortably from one foot to the other. His eyes cast downward he said, "I'm sorry, Herr Kommandant, it's…it was decided not to count them."

"Who has made this decision?" Dean's patience hung on a thin thread and his voice was sharp enough to let the other man shrink back.

"The…the…order came from the Russians. I'm sorry, but they told me—"

"I'll have a word with them," Dean interrupted the man and left, looking for Captain Orlovski. He didn't find him, but Werner Böhm was standing there together with his boss Norbert Gentner. The two Soviet stooges would have to do.

"Herr Gentner, a word please?"

The secretary general of the SED turned around, excruciatingly slowly, his face clearly showing that he wished not to talk to Dean. But Dean couldn't care less.

"You gave the order to exclude the Köpenick ballots from this election?" He attacked the man he loathed almost as much as General Sokolov.

"Herr Kommandant, the Soviet Union and the SED have the utmost interest in free and fair elections. It is a direct affront to our good relations that you would accuse us of such a thing," Gentner said in German, which Dean had only rudimentary knowledge of.

Dean looked around for his translator, but couldn't find him. Since he knew that Böhm was fluent in English, had even studied the language at the Moscow Institute of Foreign Languages, he nodded at him and said, "Herr Böhm, would you please explain to your superior that every vote will be counted in this election."

Böhm glanced at Gentner and only after the barely visible nod of the other man, he opened his mouth. "Herr Kommandant, we completely agree with your opinion, but since all bridges connecting this borough with the rest of Berlin are damaged, it's simply impossible to get the paper ballots into the city hall. Since Köpenick is located in the Soviet sector, General Sokolov has decided that we would rather withhold a few hundred votes than risk delaying the entire election. That should be in the American best interest as well, or shouldn't it?"

Dean glowered at the two SED functionaries. It was more like ten thousand votes and he knew as well as the Soviets that most of them wouldn't go to the SED. The Köpenick borough was separated from the rest of Berlin by a barrier of two rivers and a lake, so it had witnessed firsthand what it meant to belong to the Soviet-occupied zone. "What about counting the ballots over there and phoning in the results?"

A smug grin played across Böhm's lips. "This possibility was the first solution considered, but much to our chagrin, none of the telephone lines are working either. You must agree that there's nothing that can be done."

"I don't agree, and I'll personally bring the ballots over here if I must." Dean's tone of voice belied the insecurity he felt. How on earth should he make good on his promise, if the only way was crossing through the Soviet zone surrounding Berlin? He still remembered quite well the trip-from-hell with his reconnaissance unit last year.

He left Gentner and Böhm standing and went in search of his deputy. "Get me Captain Barley. Now."

Jason knew Dean well enough not to ask questions and immediately went to find a phone. Twenty minutes later Barley arrived in a military jeep.

"Colonel Harris, you wanted to see me?" Barley asked.

Dean related the situation in a few short sentences, closing with, "I need to get those ballots over here before midnight."

Barley widened his eyes. "Sir, that's two and a half hours from now. We won't be able to construct a mobile bridge across the river in such a short time, even if the Soviets allowed us…it's their sector, after all."

"Then find another solution and do it fast." Dean stared pointedly at the engineer, who cocked his head and worried his lower lip, completely ignoring his superior for a few long minutes.

"I think I know," Barley finally said. "We'll swim them across."

"What?" Dean couldn't believe his own ears. It was late October and the weather had become quite chilly. The water temperature would be around fifty degrees Fahrenheit.

"Yes. We use the narrow part at Schlossinsel, that's probably less than fifty yards. A good swimmer should have no problem getting across, strapping the ballots sealed in watertight rubber bags to his back and returning to the other side. There we'll have a jeep waiting and bring the ballots to the city hall for counting."

The idea was outrageous, but it was worth a shot. "Send someone over to organize everything with the Köpenick election board and then find as many swimmers a possible, while I take care of the Soviets."

Dean didn't even bother to talk to Gentner, because those communists could never agree to anything without General Sokolov's approval. Conveniently the general was absent and Dean phoned his office, informing the secretary, that according to the rules of quadripartite administration over Berlin he was on his way to retrieve the Köpenick ballots. He didn't divulge how exactly he planned to do this, banking on the fact that by the time Sokolov returned the call, it would be too late for the Soviets to stop the swimmers.

He felt a surge of pleasure at using the fait accompli, a favorite Russian tactic, against them.

Shortly before midnight, Captain Barley personally delivered a dozen boxes of paper ballots from Köpenick. Less than ten percent of the electorate there had voted for the SED.

CHAPTER 21

C rowds lined the streets outside the city hall, eager to find out about the election results. Marlene didn't stay to wait, because she had a date with Zara and Bruni. They would listen to RIAS Berlin at Bruni's place.

Chit-chatting about their lives, the three of them drank coffee – real coffee – and ate biscuits, all generous gifts from Feodor Orlovski. Marlene still thought it was immoral of her friend to maintain this relationship with one of the hated oppressors, but she didn't go as far as to reject the food he provided. In a Berlin riddled with food shortages that would seem downright stupid.

When the radio announcer cleared his throat, and began to speak, Marlene could see the same stunned excitement in her friends' eyes as she felt. The SED had lost by a landslide. In a massive anti-communist protest vote, especially in the Soviet sector, voter turnout had surpassed ninety percent. The clear winner with almost half of the votes was the Social Democratic Party, while the Soviet-supported SED received not even twenty percent of the votes.

"What an outstanding rebuff to a communist dictatorship," Zara said, her expression showing relief.

"A path for freedom," the announcer exclaimed. "The Berliners have voted *No* to oppression and totalitarianism and voted *Yes* to liberty and democracy. They have put the remnants of the Nazi regime into the grave once and for all, and have shown themselves a beacon of freedom for Germany, and for Eastern Europe during these dark times."

Bruni rolled her eyes, "Isn't he exaggerating a bit?"

"No, he isn't. You may not have noticed, but most everyone else in Berlin did. The Russians have abducted, arrested and done away with close to one hundred fifty thousand citizens during the past months in an attempt to suppress dissenting opinions." Zara gave her a scathing stare.

"Criminals, dangerous Nazis and other subversives," Bruni responded.

"Who's been telling you these lies? Your Russian lover?" Zara yelled.

"Please, girls, let's not get into a fight over this. We should all be happy that democracy has won. Aren't you, Bruni?" Marlene appeased her friends.

"Yes, of course I am." Bruni gracefully leaned her head to the side and offered more biscuits. But somehow Marlene had the feeling her friend wasn't all that happy.

Later in the afternoon RIAS had a four-party discussion on, and the three girls were glued to the radio. The winning Social Democrats, the Christian Democrats, the Liberal Democrats, all praised the courage of the Berliners in speaking out for freedom, a well-placed side hook to the socialists.

There was no doubt that members of the SED *Politbüro* were shocked by the outcome. Despite their having invested massive resources in the election campaign, the voters had preferred to run to the Western-backed parties.

Herr Gentner, chairman of the SED and known to be slick as an eel when responding to awkward questions, while hard as steel when pushing directives from Moscow onto the people, easily found a reason for the disaster.

"It has only been sixteen months after the downfall of Hitler's dictatorship, therefore not all the people in Germany are yet clear to know what the right way is," he stated. He never once commented on the disgusting treatment by the Russian oppressors, the gradual denial of even the most basic freedoms and the constant fear of the Berliners of being abducted by the Markgraf police, working for the NKVD.

When Marlene and Zara left Bruni's place, she embraced her friend and asked, "What will happen with your captain?" After all, he was responsible for the election campaign and thus for the catastrophic defeat.

"He'll be just fine," Bruni said with a shrug and a forced smile.

~

Werner Böhm hadn't heard or seen Orlovski since election day. Nobody ever mentioned his name again. It was almost as if he'd never existed. One day, Gentner casually mentioned that Werner needed to align with the head of engineering, Captain Ivanov.

As usual, Norbert gave his order in the usual neutral voice that didn't show the slightest trace of emotion. And Werner had been in the Soviet Union too long to even consider asking the question that burned on his tongue. *If Ivanov is the new head of engineering, what happened to Orlovski?*

Nobody ever asked questions in Russia, one waited until told what to do next. Even if the directives from today contradicted those from a week ago, no person in his right mind dared to question the sudden turn in politics.

Werner had believed this would change after the war. He'd honestly thought that Stalin's promise to "give the individual countries the freedom to go on the individual path best for them" was to be taken at face value.

But his one and a half years in Berlin had brought one disappointment after another. Slowly, almost unnoticeably, the initial liberties after the capitulation had been taken away from the German people. And the more the people resisted, the faster they saw their privileges go.

He still hoped this would change and Germany could learn from the problems in Russia and implement a better form of socialism – one that actually benefitted the people.

"Yes, Comrade, I'll take care of this immediately," he said, and walked out to find his driver. Sitting in the car, his thoughts returned to Orlovski. He couldn't say they'd been friends, but he had liked the captain's logical attitude, always keeping to facts and figures, never venturing into political discourse. "I'm an engineer," he used to say. "I can only speak about the numbers."

A sudden fear attacked Werner. Had they returned to the frightening period of the purges during the mid-thirties? When you'd wake up in the morning to find two of your best friends or family members gone?

Later in his life, during his studies at the top secret Comintern university, he'd witnessed events when students had been removed from the school after a seemingly banal mishap. One of them he'd met again six months later: a ragged, haggard, filthy man dressed in rags who begged for bread.

Perhaps this had been the turning point in his life, when he'd gone from believing in the infallibility of the system without question to secretly entertaining critical thoughts. If the party could throw a trusted long-term party member to the wolves for the slightest wrong word – he didn't even remember what his former fellow student had said – then maybe the system wasn't as perfect as it should be.

"Comrade Böhm, we've arrived," his driver said.

Captain Ivanov was the typical Red Army officer and Werner could have liked him, if he weren't the evidence for Orlovski's disappearance.

After his inaugural visit with Ivanov, he told the driver to bring him to the Café de Paris. For some reason he wanted to see Fräulein von Sinnen. Not that he expected her to know more, but maybe he wanted to make sure that Captain Orlovski had in fact existed and wasn't just an incarnation of his imagination.

As always, Fräulein von Sinnen enthused the crowd, but when her gaze fell on him, he believed he heard a slight shiver in her voice. After her performance, she came to his table.

"*Guten Abend*, Herr Böhm, would you like to order champagne for me?" she asked and gracefully sat down beside him. She was exceptionally beautiful, but he missed warmth and kindness in her personality. His heart felt a twinge as he thought of Marlene. Lively, kind, enthusiastic, honest, courageous Marlene.

"It would be my pleasure," he replied and ordered a bottle of champagne for the two of them.

Snuggling tight against him, Fräulein von Sinnen whispered into his ear, "Do you know anything about Feodor?"

Taken aback by the straightforward question, he played for time, taking a sip of champagne, before he answered, "No. And we probably never will." It was as much as he could say without entering dangerous ground.

She looked sad. "He told me never to mention his name again, should he one day disappear." Then she squared her shoulders, emptied her glass of champagne and said in her captivating voice, "Thank you so much for the company, Herr Böhm, but I must get ready for my next performance."

"It was my pleasure," he said, suddenly completely exhausted. This incident had shown him once again that he had to toe the party line at all costs. As much as he sympathized with the students and their plight for academic freedom, he had to stick to the directives.

CHAPTER 22

M arlene was leaving the lecture hall when she saw
Georg in the hallway, waving at her.

"Hey, Marlene, do you have a moment?" he asked. Beside
him stood Julian Berger, a slim and tall chemistry student with
a shock of curly blond hair.

"Sure, what's up?"

"Well, now that the elections are over and we have won—"
Georg said.

"We? I thought you're a Christian Democrat?" Marlene
interrupted him.

Julian gave her a hard look. "It doesn't matter which kind of
democrat he is, as long as he's against the communists."

Marlene rolled her eyes. This Julian was much too serious
for his own good, he never seemed to laugh and certainly
didn't understand a joke.

"So, now that the elections are over and the democratic
parties have won, we want to implement changes at the
university. But we need some more members for the student

board," Georg explained as they walked down the steps to the canteen.

"Doesn't the Board of Directors have to nominate and approve the student members?" Marlene asked and wrapped her shawl tighter around her mother's worn coat. She was beyond thankful that the university now featured a canteen that gave out one bowl of hot soup per student each day.

"Officially yes, but we are forming sub-committees that don't need official approval. Please, will you join? We need more people from the law faculty."

Marlene sighed. Taking on additional responsibilities was the last thing on her mind, but looking into Georg's pleading eyes, she simply couldn't leave him hanging, so she nodded.

"Thank you, I really appreciate your help," Georg said. "We'll have the first meeting next Monday after class." With these words he and Julian were gone, no doubt to recruit more students for their cause.

On the walk home, Marlene was pestered by second-guessing. It would be embarrassing to be so exposed. She might even have to stand up in front of an audience. Just the thought of delivering a speech like Georg had done at the inauguration earlier this year sent hot and cold shivers down her spine.

Her father would never approve. In his mind this wasn't how a girl behaved. He hadn't even wanted her to take on a leading role in Hitler's BDM – not that she'd ever voiced aspirations to do so. A sudden fury took hold of her. Ever since the downfall of the Reich she'd been the parent of the family. She'd been the one scurrying around for food, she'd braved the streets and the Russians to get ration books, new identity cards, staying permits and whatever other crazy document the Soviets wanted from them.

Should her parents disapprove, she wouldn't give up her newfound independence. Ever. She might not be comfortable in the limelight, but she would no longer hide in the background and let others make decisions for her. Not her parents, not the Soviets and certainly not Werner Böhm.

She caught herself at the thought of him and shook her head. Even after months of banning him from her mind, his handsome face still lingered, always ready to spring at her. Though not in charge of the Culture and Education department anymore, he'd begun to teach a politics class. Thus, she came across him more often than not at the university, although both of them did their best not to acknowledge the other one.

He often behaved in such a typically Russian way that she had to remind herself that he was in fact a German. He probably couldn't act as he wished but had to follow directives, too. For a moment, she even felt sorry for him. How hard it must be to be caught between two cultures, two countries, two people and two political systems.

It was already dark, but the church bells rang only five o'clock. She feared coming home to tell her parents about her new role on the student board, and thought of ways to procrastinate on her return.

My friends! She'd ask Zara and Bruni how to broach the sensitive topic. With quick steps she located the next payphone and called Bruni.

"Visit me at the club," her friend suggested. "I have an hour between my appearances. We can chat and I'll invite you for dinner when I'm through."

The mention of dinner gave the plan a whole new meaning. "How did you know I was hungry?"

"Because you're always hungry," Bruni laughed into the phone.

"Can I bring Zara, too? Because I hate going home all by myself that late at night." Even though the rapes and assaults had stopped many months ago, she still felt her skin crawl whenever a Russian soldier passed her by or, God forbid, approached her.

"Yes, bring Zara," Bruni replied. "And look nice. The club is always crawling with handsome men. You never know who you might meet."

"Oh, Bruni. You're not planning to fix us up with someone, are you?"

"No, I'm not." Bruni giggled. "See you tonight then."

Marlene ran some errands, then stole into her parents' place like a burglar, intent on meeting neither of them before she disappeared into her room. Just a few months ago they'd upgraded from the basement to a real apartment with two rooms. She took extra care with her appearance, combed her hair in the latest style and even brightened her face with a bit of makeup. In her best dress, a hand-me-down from Bruni, and her only pair of heels, she gave a happy twirl.

When she heard voices on the stairs, she moved out with lightning speed and rushed past her parents saying, "Bruni invited me for dinner."

She took the bus to Zara's place and brought her friend the happy news. As much as Zara loathed going out at night, the promise of a dinner was enough to make her brush her long ebony hair until it shone and put on the best dress she owned. Together they walked to the Café de Paris in the lovely starry night, crisp with cold foreshadowing the coming winter.

"Things look nicer at night," Marlene remarked. "The darkness hides much of the devastation.

"Yes, though have you noticed how fast some areas have been rebuilt? There's even a cinema house reopening next month," Zara said.

Marlene linked arms with her friend. "The Lichtburg. How

I loved going to the movies. What fun it will be to be able to do that again."

After a brisk thirty-minute walk they arrived at the Café de Paris, where Bruni had already announced their visit to the bouncer at the door, who directed them to Bruni's dressing room where the singer was getting ready for her first show.

"Hi, girls, how are you doing?" A very happily smiling Bruni greeted them.

"Fine, and you?" Marlene said.

"Stupendous. I have the most terrific news."

"Your captain has asked you to marry him?" Zara pursed her lips, clearly indicating she didn't consider this terrific news.

"God, no! That would be awful, wouldn't it?" Bruni hugged first Zara and then Marlene and ushered them inside. "Here we can talk privately."

Bruni offered her friends wine and chocolates with a grand pose.

"Chocolate? Did your captain get a promotion?" Marlene asked, but didn't deny herself the delicacy of a real piece of chocolate. She put it into her mouth, where it melted against her tongue, the sweet flavor exploding and sending a rush of complete and total satisfaction through her body. She groaned, "Hmmm…that's how it must feel to be in heaven."

Bruni giggled, "He did, kind of. My new benefactor is Colonel Dean Harris."

Marlene all but dropped the wine glass and stared with wide eyes at her friend. Judging by the gasp to her left, Zara was as shocked as she was.

"The American Kommandant?" Marlene whispered.

"The one and only. And he's…fantastic." Bruni made a dreamy face.

"What about Orlovski? Won't he be jealous?" Zara asked

fearfully, glancing around as if expecting to find him waiting in a corner.

"Oh, Zara, I thought you're so politically interested. Haven't you heard?" Bruni asked.

"Heard what?"

"That he left Berlin."

Marlene cocked her head. "Actually, I've been wondering, because I heard nothing of him since the elections."

Bruni gave a theatrical sigh. "He might have been promoted. I don't know. About a week before he left, he told me not to ask questions and never again mention his name in case he should disappear."

Marlene felt the shock seeping deep into her bones. *A promotion?* That must be the joke of the century. More probably he'd joined the thousands of abducted Berliners at whatever location where the Soviets kept their enemies of the state. And Orlovski clearly had become an enemy by not winning them the elections.

"You just move on?" Zara wondered.

"Come on, Zara, you of all persons feel sorry for him? I thought you never liked him."

"I didn't, but that's no reason to drop him like a hot potato," Zara hissed, her eyes shining with righteous indignation.

"I didn't drop him, remember? I'm still here. He was the one to leave. It's time to look into the future, and an American Kommandant is so much more powerful. More money, better gifts, even better rations. And he's so much more virile...you know..."

"God, spare us the gory details." Marlene wrinkled her nose in distaste at her friend's candor and lack of any sort of moral compass.

"An American is preferable to a Russian, I suppose," Zara

said naively. "Not that I would share a bed with an Allied soldier. They came here as occupiers, not to be our friends."

"It takes all sorts." Bruni was in too good a mood to be put down.

"At least he won't disappear overnight; the Americans don't send their people to Siberia, like the Russians do," Marlene said.

"Shushh…never talk about that or you might be the next one on their list," Bruni warned them.

Which is exactly the reason never to get involved with a communist, Marlene thought to herself.

A knock on the door summoned Bruni to the stage. Marlene and Zara were escorted by the manager himself, who walked them through a sea of appreciative men, to a reserved table in the elegant nightclub.

Bruni was announced amid a drumroll and a flurry of claps and wolf whistles. This was her natural environment and she glowed in the spotlight that set her apart from her audience. The music began to play and a hushed silence spread through the room. She started to sing, and at the end of her chanson the room burst into thunderous applause.

Marlene admired the way Bruni knew exactly how to play her audience, while Marlene herself would have died of embarrassment should anyone order her to climb on the stage and sing.

Not Bruni. She smiled, blew kisses, waved to familiar faces, and flirted with the men, as she moved seductively around the stage. On the stage was a star, a gifted woman. It was no wonder she was a regular act at the Café de Paris while other performers came and went.

"Sitting in the corner are two of my best friends," Bruni announced, peering through the darkened room and pointing out Marlene and Zara. "This is their first visit to our Café de Paris, so be nice, boys."

A roar of applause followed the spotlight that singled out the two embarrassed women. Marlene felt her face flush with heat, but she somehow managed to give a polite wave and swore to murder Bruni later.

Bruni returned to her dressing room to change while the band played the latest popular songs. Some of the GIs fascinated onlookers with their gravity-defying jive moves, a dance craze that captivated the younger crowd.

A couple of Russian soldiers came up to Marlene and Zara, asking for a dance but they politely declined, too shy to make a spectacle of themselves with their lack of ability on the dance floor. The men weren't pleased and since they had obviously had a bit too much to drink, they insisted rather stubbornly on this dance.

Marlene felt completely at the mercy of these louts and helplessly glanced at Zara, who didn't seem more confident either, when out of the blue, Werner Böhm and another well-dressed young civilian stood in front of her. As much as she wanted to avoid him, she couldn't help but give him her brightest smile.

Werner said something in Russian to the two soldiers, who quickly disappeared, and then he asked, "Would you grant me this dance, please?"

Much to her surprise, she heard someone say, "It would be my pleasure."

She glanced around, but Zara was already on the way to the dance floor with the other man. Before Marlene even realized that it was herself, who'd given her consent, Werner put an arm around her waist and led her through the crowd.

The weight of his arm seared through her clothes, making her skin tingle and her legs go to jelly. All the resolve to keep away from him had been crushed with one single smile. He was a gifted dancer and guided her masterfully between the other couples. After fighting the intoxicating sensation for a while, she decided to give in to it and enjoy being held in his arms.

"We should go back now," Marlene stuttered, when the song ended.

"Yes, of course, if that's what you wish," he replied gracefully. Leaning over, he touched her cheek with his as he said, "Thank you for the dance, Marlene." Then his firm hand on her back led her to their table, where Bruni and dinner were already waiting for them.

Bruni gave Böhm a brilliant smile, but as soon as he'd excused himself, she pounced on Marlene. "What's going on between the two of you?"

"Nothing."

"So why the silly smitten look on his face – and on yours?" Bruni's power of observation was sharp as a knife.

"I don't fancy Werner at all, but—" Marlene tried to form an excuse to satisfy her friends.

"One dance and it's Werner, is it?" Bruni laughed, delighted by Marlene's slip-up. "Admit it, you're in love with the detestable Werner Böhm."

"Stop being ridiculous!" Marlene blushed. "He is a gentleman, nothing more and nothing less. I've always admitted that he has impeccable manners. And he really did save us from a most embarrassing situation."

Zara now joined Bruni's laughter, because she evidently had been able to dance with Böhm's friend without flushing like a pumpkin.

"Stop it, will you! Or someone will hear your nonsensical accusations," Marlene pleaded with them.

At last her friends changed the subject and the time flew by while they ate their dinner. As soon as they finished, Bruni had to go on stage for another performance and Werner seemed to have waited for just this moment, because he came to their table to ask for another dance.

Marlene agreed, because there was nothing wrong in dancing with him, right? She enjoyed the second dance even more than the first one, feeling already strangely at home in his arms. She didn't have to engage her mind anymore to follow his lead, it was as if her body already knew the upcoming steps.

When the music paused, she returned to their table, out of breath from the vigorous dancing, but happier than she'd been in a long time.

Zara saw her heated face and said, "Marlene, I shall go home now. I have to get up early in the morning. But you, by all means, should stay and have fun."

"No way. We came here together and we'll return home together as well. What kind of friend would I be to send you home all alone this late at night?" Marlene answered and grabbed her handbag.

"Please ladies, allow me to drop you home," Werner suggested, and seeing the hesitation in their eyes he added, "I have a car at my disposal."

Marlene reluctantly accepted his generous offer. It's not that she was afraid of him, but more of herself and her lack of self-control in his presence. He dropped off Zara first and then headed into the Russian sector for Marlene's home.

Throughout the journey, they didn't speak a word, but the tension crackled in the car. She was grateful for the darkness that enveloped them and hid her expression from him.

"Is this your place?" he said, surprise in his voice.

"Yes," Marlene said in a low tone as she saw the dilapidated building for the first time through the eyes of a man who lived in one of the few undestroyed boroughs in Berlin, a requisitioned apartment in Pankow he shared with another member of the Gentner group.

He walked around the car and opened the door for her. "I'll walk you to your door. You can never be too careful around here."

She actually welcomed his company, not because she was afraid of an attack, but because she yearned to prolong the time with him just a bit more.

"Thank you for driving me home," she said, looking up at him. The keys in her hand began to jingle as she stared into his mesmerizing green eyes. His face looked so young, so innocent, so honest.

"May I kiss you?" he asked and when she didn't protest, he leaned down and pressed his warm lips on hers.

Against her better judgement, she opened her lips and returned the kiss. A heated minute later, she stepped back and whispered, "I… should go."

"Good night, my sweet Marlene." The words from his mouth caused a myriad of butterflies to flutter in her stomach and she hurriedly unlocked the door and rushed inside.

Damn him! Why did she like him so much?

CHAPTER 23

D ean watched the beautiful blonde by his side. Bruni von Sinnen was really something. Not only did she possess fantastic looks, but she knew how to please in bed. The best thing about her, though, was that she didn't succumb to girlish notions of love, but looked at their relationship for what it was. A pleasant business.

The life of the American Kommandant in Berlin was a lonely one. The Berlin population oscillated between loathing and admiring him. The entire Russian military, spearheaded by General Sokolov, equated him with a beast and called him Enemy of Democracy. He constantly received anonymous death threats and had slept with a pistol under his pillow for the past one and a half years.

Sure, his subordinates respected him, but he could never confide his sorrows to anyone, except maybe at times to his deputy and friend Jason Gardner.

Bruni provided him with much-needed comfort and everything else a man needed who hadn't seen his own wife in almost four years. In exchange, he provided for her, protected her, and allowed her to live a better life than the other Berliner Fräuleins. It truly was a win-win situation.

He kissed her goodbye and slipped out of bed in the dark of the night to return to his own quarters.

In the morning, his deputy was already waiting for him in his office.

"Morning, Jason, what's up?"

Jason grimaced. "The Soviets giving us problems."

"Tell me something new." Dean settled at his desk and beckoned for his friend to take a place opposite him. "What's it this time?"

"Sokolov issued an order that none of the members of the Magistrat who were elected last month are allowed to take their position without prior approval of the Kommandatura."

Dean slammed his fist on the desk with such force that the old wood creaked. "Why don't I know about this?"

"I just found out," Jason said. "Since he's the current chairman he issued the order without consulting the others first."

Dean's fist was still hurting or he'd have slammed it on the desk again. "How dare this filthy, lying, crooked asshole! He doesn't have the authority to issue such orders."

"Sir, it gets worse," Jason looked at him, obviously loathing his situation of having to relay more bad news. On Dean's nod he began to explain, "The newly elected members have complained about communist squads being trucked to the City Hall to beat them up."

"That must be a joke."

"It's not."

Dean called his secretary, "Get me Sokolov on the line. Immediately." It was barely ten a.m., so Sokolov would still be fast asleep. "Oh, don't bother," Dean said. "Tell him I'm coming to his office at noon and he'd better be there or I'll give him hell."

"You know there's not that much you can do, right?" Jason asked him.

He sighed. The City Hall, the Magistrat and the City Council, all of them were in the Soviet sector. Technically Sokolov's cronies could do to the people in their sector as they pleased and nobody, not even the American Kommandant, could hold them accountable for their crimes.

In the Kommandatura the three Western Allies had made every effort to work with the Soviets. In the beginning, they'd acquiesced to every Russian whim, hoping the other party would see the honest will to cooperate. When this didn't work, they'd accepted, against their better judgement, unfavorable and crooked terms. They'd appeased the gangsters like an abused wife might appease her husband, all in an attempt to show their goodwill and honest dedication to govern Berlin together – and to prevent another war. That the Soviets might start another war was the biggest fear of everyone in the West and dictated the odd appeasement policy.

But the daily obstruction of the Soviets took a toll on Dean, and more than once he he'd grabbed the phone to ask General Clay for a transfer away from the city of hell, although he never actually completed the call.

Almost six weeks after the election, the new city government was still unseated. The despicable Russians kept the old SED-dominated administration in place, while allegedly investigating some of the new candidates for Nazi crimes, and there was nothing Dean could do about it.

CHAPTER 24

For three weeks after the night when he had dropped Marlene off at her home, Werner persisted, taking every opportunity to meet with her and using his charm to woo her. Eventually, she relented and they became a couple, meeting clandestinely two or three times each week

He should be happy, but a nagging sorrow ate at him. The party would never approve of their relationship, because Marlene was not a trusted communist and he, well, he was one of the highest SED functionaries in Berlin.

Every so often he toyed with the idea of defying the party. But then, menacing old memories resurfaced and drowned out the thought. He knew better than to challenge his superiors since such a move would mark the end of both Marlene and him. He certainly didn't want to share the same mysterious fate as Captain Orlovski. Yet there was no way he was going to give up Marlene either.

He thought up a solution and the next time they met, he said as casually as possible, "Why don't you join the SED?"

"What?" She glared daggers at him and before she could scratch out his eyes, he raised his hands in a placatory way.

"Please, hear me out. It would be much better and we could openly show our love." He showered her with the charming smile that always made her purr like a kitten.

Not today.

"Better for whom?" she said with a scathing voice. "And why? Do you have to get approval from Comrade Gentner or General Sokolov on who you're going out with?"

Not exactly – although he did have to follow the party line, and that didn't include a romantic relationship with a woman who wasn't a trusted comrade. "Don't be silly, Marlene. Of course not, but in the current political climate it wouldn't be beneficial for me to be seen fraternizing with members of the opposition," Werner explained gently. At the sight of her furiously shimmering eyes he hastily added, "And it might tarnish your good name."

"Member of the opposition?" she exclaimed. "I'm not even a party member."

"No, you're not, *mein Liebling*," he replied, kissing her cheek. "I suggest this move only because it's in your best interest. Both of our best interests. Your anti-Soviet stance has been noted. If we want to be together, we cannot be on opposite sides; the SED won't stand for it."

"Surely one is allowed to have opinions?" Marlene said hotly.

Actually not. At least not when they deviate from the official party line. He inwardly cursed the SED leaders for their stupidity. For everyone but Norbert it was clear that the catastrophic loss in the elections last year had been due to the SED's reputation as being the "Soviet party".

But instead of changing course and insisting on an independent socialist way for Germany, blockheaded Gentner and his closest cronies had stuck their noses way up into the Soviet asses.

"Of course, you are entitled to your own opinion, and the SED leaders together with the Soviet occupation power wholeheartedly supported the free and fair elections in Berlin. But in our case, it is like one person trying to build a house, while the other person tries to knock it down."

He pondered whether to muzzle her protest with a lengthy dialectic lecture about the philosophical background of Marxism-Leninism, but opted against it. It would only help to enrage her more. Since Marlene wasn't a schooled and trained party official, she reacted to theoretical lectures like most lay people did: rolling her eyes and an outright refusal to even consider the truth behind his words.

"What a terrible analogy," Marlene gasped. "Now I'm the one obstructing the rebuilding of Berlin when in fact these hideous Russians disassemble what's left right from under our noses."

Werner sighed. He didn't approve of the demolition for reparations either, he'd even tried to talk to Norbert about this. But in his arrogant manner Norbert had simply stated that the topic wasn't to be discussed. Ever. Again.

"I know, it seems unjust, but we always have to remember how much our Russian friends suffered at the hands of the Nazis—"

"They're not *my* Russian friends," Marlene scoffed, turned on her heel, and walked out on him.

He stared at her, angry about her insolence, but at the same time envious. He wished he could do the same, just once, and walk out of yet another ludicrous party meeting where the comrades tried to outdo each other in kissing Moscow's ass.

Then he gave a start at the critical thought. Had his discontent with the party evolved so far already? Despite the many things he disliked about Stalinism, he still harbored the highest hopes for a new and better way in Germany.

But the future looked bleaker and bleaker.

CHAPTER 25

Georg, Marlene, Lotte, and Julian were butting heads in a heated discussion at Georg's place.

"I tell you we need to be more aggressive," Julian said.

"That's not a good idea, you heard the Board of Directors. The administration unfortunately cannot give in to our requests, because their hands are tied." Georg was being the voice of reason.

"Their hands are tied? Don't make me laugh! The SED is high up the Soviet asses, fearing for their privileges and *pajoks* if they say a single wrong word." Julian's eyes shimmered with rage. While the rest of Berliners suffered hunger and lack of housing, clothes, even paper and pens, the SED functionaries lived in nice villas requisitioned from former Nazis.

Marlene had never been to Werner's place, but she knew that he'd chosen a more modest four-room-apartment that he shared with another bachelor. At least Werner also disapproved of the blatant disparity between Berliners and party members and officials. According to him, that was in direct opposition to Marx's teachings.

The *pajoks* were regular weekly or monthly boxes filled with all the goods, food and others one couldn't buy on the open market, or even on the black market. Werner had often given her the ingredients of his box, since he got to eat at the canteen in the SED headquarters, the *Haus der Einheit*.

"How do you know about the *pajoks*?" Marlene asked, since they were never officially mentioned.

"Everyone knows, despite the Soviets' intention to keep their bribery a secret," Julian said.

"They're not bribes, they're a system to help the most hard-working people who are needed for the rebuilding of our city." Marlene felt the need to defend Werner, even though he wasn't personally accused. "These people simply don't have the time and energy to queue up for rations."

Lotte rolled her eyes. "You don't really believe this yourself, now do you? Otherwise why are these *pajoks* handed out based on rank and honor in the supposedly classless Soviet system? Why aren't they given to the hard-working industrial workers? Or the construction workers who rebuilt the railway tracks the Russians have dismantled?"

"Can we please get back to the topic at hand?" Georg called them to order.

"I say, we need to let those goons know that we're not willing to live under the Soviet thumb. This is Berlin, not the Soviet-occupied zone," Julian exclaimed.

"We could ask the other Allied powers for help maybe? Since they govern us quadripartite…" Lotte suggested.

Julian scoffed. "The Western Allies are useless, all they do is bow to the Soviet antics in some misguided effort to appease them. And … since when are the Americans our friends?"

"They could be. Don't you see how they're honestly trying to help us rebuild our country? After all, we were the ones to run it into the ground by following Hitler and fighting everyone else," Lotte said.

"Not me," Julian growled.

"So what? You aren't the only one in this room who was in a concentration camp."

Marlene perked up her ears. Had everyone except her been in a camp?

"Please, can you guys keep focused on our topic?" Georg was getting desperate.

"We could write a petition, signed by all of us and present it to the Culture and Education department," Marlene suggested, since she knew how much the SED officials loved written papers. Most everything they did was introduced via a petition and resolved by a resolution.

"It's a good idea," Georg said without much enthusiasm.

"I'm so sorry," Lotte said hesitantly. "I can't do this."

"Why not? Don't you want the communists to keep their filthy fingers out of our education?" Julian sprung up and paced the room.

"I can't go up against the Russians," Lotte explained. "My boyfriend is still in a Soviet prisoner-of-war camp. He's supposed to be released soon, so I can't do anything that will jeopardize Johann's release."

Marlene shook her head. "Please, Lotte, do you really think the Russians would hold your boyfriend accountable for your actions?"

Lotte stared at her in disbelief. "Tell me, where exactly do you live? Don't you ever read the news or is all your information coming from Böhm?"

Marlene shot her friend a furious glare. She shouldn't have confided in Lotte that she and Werner had been a couple for several months now. Thankfully, Julian was too enraged to even notice Lotte's slip-up.

"What I see is a coward, Lotte. Isn't it a very convenient time to bring up a mysterious boyfriend nobody has ever seen?" Julian said scathingly.

"You're a pompous asshole! Nobody has seen him for the very reason that the bloody Russians have kept him prisoner for the past two and a half years," Lotte yelled and sprang to her feet, almost colliding with the pacing Julian.

"Calm down." Georg's deep voice interrupted the fight. "We need to present a united front. Because it's only in solidarity that we can engineer a change. Nothing will happen to any of us."

Lotte turned around to give Georg her full attention. "Look, I have learned the hard way that sometimes it's better to keep my mouth shut. And now is one of those times. I, for myself, am not going to endanger Johann's life by signing this petition."

"The Russians aren't like the Nazis, Lotte," Georg replied softly. "There's no need for you to be so afraid of them."

"Oh? There isn't? Tell that to the hundred thousand who've been abducted, beaten, harassed, threatened and sent to camps during the election campaign last year? Are you all blind, deaf and dumb? Don't you read the newspaper? Don't you know about the nightly social visits by the Markgraf police? And how the visited people either disappear without a trace or are never the same again? Do you all really not know about this? Or do you just close your eyes?" Lotte was talking herself into a rage.

"Of course we know." Georg stood up, as if he wanted to prevent Lotte from physically attacking Julian. Or maybe from storming out of the room. "But this is the very reason we have to stand united. Only in great numbers are we strong."

Lotte shook her head. "I'm sorry, but I just can't. Not right now." Then she left the room, leaving the other three looking after her – Julian furious, Georg sad, and Marlene worried.

"We don't need the spineless worm," Julian said and returned to the table. "Now, what are we going to write for the petition?"

Marlene looked at the closed door through which her friend had walked seconds before and wished she could have left with her. But she stayed, because she didn't want to disappoint Georg and Julian.

The two of them barely noticed her as they drafted the petition, meant to change the lives of the students in Berlin.

"There comes a time when we must do what our conscience tells us is right," Julian said, putting the last sentence on a piece of paper.

"Those in power may try to ignore us, but if there are enough protesters, then they will be forced to address our requests," Georg said.

She listened to the men spout their rhetoric, but she had a bad feeling about all of this. The SED-dominated university leadership had dismissed their requests the year before, why would they now be open to them?

CHAPTER 26

Werner took Marlene on a trip into the outskirts of Berlin, where they could spend time together without being seen by anyone. He felt shoddy for hiding her, but convinced himself it was for the best – his and hers. As long as the stubborn woman didn't join the SED it wasn't sensible to be seen with her in public.

Politics never left them alone and while walking along the lake, Marlene complained about the arrogant dismissal of the students' petition. Werner had heard about the thing and sympathized with the students. None of their requests were unreasonable. They simply wanted less Soviet influence on their lives and studies.

But that ship had sailed a year ago. Now, in summer 1947, Gentner had tightened the rule and tied his party even closer to Moscow. In fact, the true rulers of the SED, the Soviet-occupied zone, and by extension Berlin, was the Soviet Military Administration. The task of the German government was simply to explain and defend the Russian decisions to the people.

He couldn't tell her that, though. Instead he said, "If the Culture and Education department can't fulfill your requests, then I'm afraid nothing can be done, since the officials have their directives to follow."

"You and your directives," she said.

"Darling, please, as much as I can understand your frustration, it's time to stop engaging in this useless fight."

She glared daggers at him. "Actually, it is exactly the time to continue. If we give up now, the Russians will steamroll over us and we'll never see the light of day again."

He gave a deep sigh and stopped to take her hands into his. "Openly opposing the reigning power is never a good thing."

"Ah...now it isn't? But two years ago, your people damned us for not openly opposing the Nazis!" Marlene spat out the words with such a fury, it was like a punch to his gut. A well-deserved one.

"This is completely different..." His defense was as lame as they came, because in fact nothing was different. Had he not secretly applauded the few valiant comrades who'd dared to stand up to Gentner? Had he not rooted for the old Bolsheviks who'd formed the illegal resistance in Germany? And had he not hoped their indomitable fighting spirit and independent thinking would bring a fresh wind into the party?

Having come to Germany with the highest hopes of an individual way to socialism, one that omitted the mistakes made in Russia and didn't submissively implement everything Stalin said, he now stood in front of the woman he loved with all his hopes shattered.

But his brain, indoctrinated with the principles of Stalinism and party discipline for half a lifetime, wouldn't let him break free. Therefore he lied to Marlene, "...It's just a transitional period. Soon, when the after-war chaos is resolved, there'll be more liberties for everyone."

"You are full of bullshit," she said and took up their walk again. After a few minutes of silence, she added, "Let's not talk about politics, shall we?"

"I promise," he said and placed a kiss on her lips. "This day is much too beautiful to ruin it. What do you want to do now?"

∼

In the evening Werner dropped Marlene off at her place and then returned to his apartment in Pankow. His roommate and good friend, Horst, greeted him with the words, "Comrade, you're lucky that you're not assigned to the university anymore."

"Why's that?" Werner responded in his most blasé voice, despite the fact that his heart had just plummeted into his boots.

"You won't believe it. I'm sure the Americans are behind all of this, but this stupid student board just announced that they're not going to accept our dismissal of their requests and are going to demonstrate against the influence of communist propaganda in their subjects."

Werner felt all the blood drain from his face and he had to put a hand against the wall to steady himself. *Marlene hasn't said a word. Doesn't she trust me?* The thought stabbed deep into his heart but at the same time he had to suppress a bitter laugh. He never told her anything, either.

"That is a very grave disregard of the authorities. What will happen now?" Werner asked as nonchalantly as he could muster. Not even Horst knew Marlene's identity. He only knew about the existence of a German girl.

"Oh man, Gentner was furious. You know him, his voice could have cut an iceberg into pieces. He literally said that once students think they can get away with such anarchy, they will strike whenever they please. The university will become a hotbed of political activity and this is certainly not the objective of this prestigious academy. Then he promised grave consequences."

"Criticism and self-criticism with dismissal from the university for the main perpetrators?" Werner asked. This was an often-used method of the communist party in the Soviet Union to criticize and punish a comrade for anti-party sentiments actually committed or – more often than not – perceived. He'd been the victim of several of these sessions, which could last for many hours, and it was a soul-crashing experience. Each time he'd felt lower than the dirt beneath his fingernails.

"No. Gentner said this wouldn't work, because these subversives aren't communists. They would only gloat when asked about their crimes. Proactive measures are required. Something more effective to solve the problem once and for all." Horst lowered his voice. "I shouldn't even tell you. A list of all members of the student board was handed over to the Markgraf police."

It took all of Werner's strength not to tear his eyes wide open. In an effort not to seem too interested, he said, "And when is this planned?"

"Tonight." Horst said, apparently uncomfortable with the sinister things he knew would soon happen. "By the way, have you heard that Gentner's petition to stop the dismantling of German industries has been granted and there will be an official celebration thanking the Soviets for their generosity and their friendship with the German people?"

"That truly is an achievement," Werner said, although he wanted to vomit at Gentner's bootlicking attitude. Friendship for the Soviet nation and acceptance of their role as the first socialist country was one thing, but brown-nosing Moscow?

For a promise to stop dismantling industry that was crucial for the rebuilding of Germany? A promise the Americans and British had implemented months ago? He urgently needed to be alone to think.

"I'm sorry, Horst, I need to study some pamphlets for tomorrow." He excused himself and went to his room. Norbert had made it clear that not the slightest independent thinking would be tolerated among the students. Judging by the grave expression on Horst's face, he feared the worst. Horrible memories assaulted him. Had it come this far already? Would the SED in their quest to mimic everything the Soviets did also repeat the bleak times of the Great Purge during the mid-thirties?

Werner shuddered. There had been abductions and arrests last year during the election campaign. But incarcerating anti-fascist students was another step down into the hell of Stalinism.

Hell of Stalinism? My God, what am I thinking? He was truly disturbed by his heretical thoughts. Stalinism might have some flaws – that nobody ever talked about for fear of being sent to Siberia – but it was still the leading implementation of Marxism-Leninism and thus a good thing.

He paced the room, fear making him short of breath. In his mind he went through the list of student board members, although he didn't indulge in any illusions that he could save anyone on the list. Julian was the ringleader, and lived in the Russian sector, so he was probably lost. Lotte had resigned from the board weeks ago, so she should be safe. Georg – hot and cold shudders ran down his spine. Norbert had ordered him to become friends with Georg. Did this mean Georg's behavior would now fall back on him? Probably not, but any attempt to spare the young man from the police sweep would directly indict Werner.

His stomach tied itself into a knot as he thought of the calm, upright, honest young man and his own inability to prevent what the police held in store for him. Then he remembered that Georg lived in the American sector and relief flushed his system. The Americans didn't take kindly to these kinds of assaults in their territory, so Georg was probably safe.

But the moment his thoughts turned to Marlene hot fear rushed through his veins. Albeit keeping in the background, she was still a member of the board and she lived in the Soviet sector. He could not let anything happen to her.

Deeply troubled, he cursed himself for falling in love with this stubborn woman who just didn't realize what was good for her. If she had joined the SED like he'd suggested, this wouldn't even be a problem.

You have to calm down, there's nothing you can do. They aren't after her, she's just a nominal member, he tried to console himself. It didn't work. Another pesky voice asked, *What if they take her? What if they send her to some prison camp? To Siberia? Could you live with the fact that you didn't even try to save her?*

He could not.

He had to come up with a plan.

CHAPTER 27

I t was almost dinner time when a knock came on the door. Marlene looked at her parents, but neither of them was expecting visitors.

"Go get it," her father said.

Marlene almost fell backwards when Werner stood in front of the door with a grave expression on his face, looking ridiculous in a trench coat and a French beret.

"What on earth…" she said, but Werner put his finger across his lips urging her to be silent.

"I need to talk to you. Tell your parents you're visiting a sick friend," he whispered.

She rolled her eyes, but obeyed. "Mother, Father, I'm needed at the hospital. I'll be back soon," she told her parents, and grabbed her coat.

"What's going on? Why this ridiculous beret?" she snapped at him.

"Because we're going to a French restaurant, my love. I'm sorry about our argument earlier and want to make it up to you."

She cast him a suspicious glance, but didn't say anything. Subsisting on meager rations one did not turn down an invitation to dinner, to a French restaurant no less, out of pride. When Werner kissed her she was overwhelmed by her love for him, and forgot his strange behavior.

He took her to a restaurant in the French sector that was well known for its fine cuisine. In the dimly lit room, she felt like a princess, attended by a myriad of waiters and Werner himself. He could be the most charming, kind, and warm-hearted man when he wanted, but she also knew his cold and distant side – when he had to push nonsensical political directives on the people.

As much as she loved him, she wished he could free himself from decade-long indoctrination and see the Soviet way for what it was: the cruel oppression of the people in a shameless effort to line the pockets of a few lucky fat cats.

"Do you want some more wine?" Werner asked her, his handsome face close to hers.

She nodded, inhaling his fresh scent, itching to reach out her fingers and let them glide across the shaven face.

As the evening progressed, he paid the bill and then said to her, "Come with me, I want to show you something."

Marlene was slightly tipsy with the bottle of wine they'd shared and all the attention she'd received. It was slightly chilly outside, but Werner put his arm around her shoulders and his nearness gave her warmth.

They walked to a hotel not far from the restaurant and she couldn't believe it when he stepped inside and told the cheerful receptionist in French, "A room in the name of Private Etoile."

"Oui, Monsieur," she smiled, her French even worse than Marlene's. "We have your booking."

Werner switched to German. "Thank you, Fräulein. The champagne..."

179

"Yes, Monsieur Etoile, it has been delivered to your room just as you ordered," the receptionist said. Apparently, she was used to French soldiers coming here to spend the night with their German Fräuleins.

Marlene couldn't stop wondering. No questions asked, no ID cards required. It was almost as if the hotel owner preferred not to know about the guests. Suddenly her heart pounded in her chest. It was absolutely inappropriate to be alone with Werner in a hotel room this late at night, and any decent girl should leave right now.

But she didn't. In truth, she had yearned for months to go further than exchanging a few stolen kisses here and there. She longed to be alone with him and feel his body pressed against hers. To savor his kisses and explore how it felt to lie together. As soon as he locked the door behind them, they fell into each other's arms.

"I've wanted to do this for months, my darling," Werner said as he rained kisses all over her face.

"Me, too," Marled murmured, but all of her words and thoughts ceased to exist the moment his lips touched hers. She was thrown into the sheer magic of love. There was no need for words to express their feelings. Not the good ones and certainly not the bad ones. His kisses were a promise of a bright future, where they could be together forever.

Their first night together was exquisite. Werner was a wonderful lover and she responded passionately to his touch. By the early hours of the morning the champagne bottle was empty and the couple exhausted. Drunk on love, Marlene fell into a deep sleep.

$\backsim$

She woke in the morning, surprised to find herself alone in the room. She rolled over to Werner's side of the bed, but it was cold. Then her gaze fell on the note lying on the nightstand.

"I realize now that passion is not love. It's not going to work out between us, we are too different people," the note said. "Please don't try to contact me again. This is for both our sakes."

Anger took over and she imagined strangling him after scratching out his eyes. The money he'd left for her on the nightstand made her feel used and dirty. It tainted the wonderful experience of the previous night.

"What a fool I've been. How dare you treat me like this?" she shouted at the walls that discreetly kept their silence.

The chimes of a nearby clock tower reminded her of the time, and she jumped up and frantically got dressed. Her parents must be worried, wondering where she'd been all night. Her parents!

Sheer panic crept up her spine. If her father knew what she'd done, he'd beat her to a pulp. She needed to come up with an alibi, and quick. Bruni – no, that wouldn't work, since her father despised the singer for her lose morals. Dr. Ebert – no, she didn't want him to lie for her. Zara! Yes, Zara lived nearby in the French sector and despite her father's newfound hate for Zara's father, she was still an acceptable character witness.

She rounded the corner into Zara's street the moment her friend left her house.

"Hey, Zara!"

"Hey, Marlene. What are you doing here this early in the morning?" Zara hugged her.

"I need to ask you a favor. I...can you...in case my parents ask..." Marlene felt her ears burning with shame.

Zara took one scrutinizing look at Marlene's face and

giggled. "You had a secret rendezvous? Let me guess…with Herr Böhm?"

Heat emanated from Marlene's face, giving away her secret. "It's not what you think. We broke up."

"I'm sorry," Zara said. "So, what am I supposed to do?"

"Just in case my parents ask, will you please tell them I spent the night with you? Because it got late and I was afraid to return home alone?"

"No problem. And hey, if you want to talk…"

"No thanks. We talked. We quit. There's nothing more to say." Marlene would not tell even her best friends about the shameful experience of this morning. Nobody would ever find out, and for all she was concerned, Werner Böhm never existed. Traitorous scum. He wasn't worth shedding a single tear over.

When Marlene got home she found her mother in tears and her father in a furious rage.

"I'm so sorry. It got late and I spent the night at Zara's place —" she began.

"Thank God you did," her mother sobbed. "The Markgraf police came for you last night. Why, Marlene? What have you done?"

"You have to resign from the student board. I allowed you to study, not to meddle in politics," her father shouted.

"I will," she said half-heartedly. Right now, she had more urgent problems. Shaken to the core, she rushed to Georg's place. His sister opened the door, visibly distraught when Marlene asked about him.

"He's not here. He received a call last night to visit Erich over in Kreuzberg and hasn't returned home since," his sister said.

The icy hand of deathlike fear squeezed Marlene's heart and froze the blood in her veins. "Thanks, I'll get in touch when I find out something," she told Georg's sister and turned on her heels.

What now? Check on Julian? Better not, since he lived in the Soviet sector. The abductions usually took place at night, but even in broad daylight, Marlene didn't feel safe right now. She decided to pay Lotte a visit. Maybe she knew something.

By the time she arrived at Lotte's apartment, the grapevine had done its work and Lotte frantically wrapped her arms around Marlene. "Thank God, you're okay."

"You have heard?" Marlene asked.

"Yes, it's awful. In total a dozen student leaders, all of them not members of the SED, have disappeared last night. Julian, Georg, Klaus, and Sandra, among them," Lotte said in a hoarse voice. "We thought, you too."

Marlene's feet suddenly gave out under her and Lotte dragged her inside to flop onto the sofa.

"I...I happened to spend the night at Zara's because it got late..." A thought entered her mind, but the idea was too absurd to even consider it.

"Lucky girl. Looks like you have a resourceful guardian angel," Lotte said and brought Marlene tea. "Here, drink this for the shock. You had better not go home, at least for a few days, until the dust has settled."

Marlene nodded in a haze, her brain not really up to the task of processing a rational thought.

"...and don't go to university either. Don't enter the Soviet sector." Lotte looked at her with a sorrowful face. "You know how wicked the Russians are. They never try an accused person, because the moment you're accused by the party, you're already guilty, since there's no room for error. The only thing remaining is to determine your punishment."

Completely traumatized, Marlene thanked Lotte for her advice and took a bus to the French sector where Bruni lived.

The quick-witted and well-connected woman would know what to do.

It was almost noon when she arrived and Marlene kept ringing the bell until a tousled Bruni finally appeared in her nightgown.

"What the hell, Marlene?" Bruni growled, but stopped when she saw the stricken look on her friend's face. "Come in. But you'd better have a good reason for this. If you've woken me to whine about a lovers' quarrel, I'm going to kill you."

Trembling, she told Bruni what had happened during the last twenty hours.

As always Bruni was quick to assess the facts and find the hidden connections. "Wow! Böhm must have known about the upcoming raid."

Marlene had her own suspicious about this already, but she still denied it. "No, I don't believe he did. He's not in the education department anymore."

Bruni waved her argument away with a graceful movement of her hand. "It's the only explanation for his otherwise very peculiar behavior. Why else would he show up on your doorstep after spending the day with you, wearing a French beret and taking you to the French sector? Seducing you to spend the night with him? Was he any good, by the way?"

"Bruni!" Marlene protested. "That's completely beside the point."

"But I'd still like to know." Bruni made a dreamy face. "I've had many men, but never a German émigré to Moscow. I'd really love to know how they compare. Does he make love like a German or like a Russian?"

"I'm not going to tell you," Marlene all but yelled at her friend. "Suppose he knew, why didn't he just tell me? He didn't have to seduce me just to save my life."

"Do you ever listen to yourself?" Bruni laughed. "You

wouldn't have believed him. You'd have wanted to prove that there's law and order in Berlin and stayed at home."

Marlene shrugged. Her friend might be on to something. Not that she'd ever admit it. But Werner obviously knew her well enough to suspect that she'd never have listened to him. "It still wasn't the right thing to do."

"You're furious because he saved your life?" Bruni asked, tossing her blond hair behind her shoulder.

"Yes, I am. He doesn't love me, he just slept with me to save my life. How cruel is this?"

Bruni couldn't hold back her laughter and giggled, "Personally I think that's a great reason to sleep with someone." Then her expression sobered and she added, "Why on earth did you become a student leader? No, don't tell me, you were pushed into it and couldn't say no."

"Yes, that's about it. You know me too well," Marlene answered with a subdued voice.

"You do realize you're in a lot of trouble, right? We should visit the military administration and clear your name, since you can't be on the run indefinitely."

"No, I can't. What if they're still looking for me?" Marlene gasped.

"Be glad that you have me," Bruni smiled. "Major Dengin owes me a favor. Now first, I want you to write a letter." She sat Marlene down at a table with paper and a pen and began to dictate…

True to her word, Bruni accompanied Marlene into the Russian sector and called on Major Dengin, who attended to them immediately.

"Fräulein von Sinnen, it's always a pleasure to see you, but what brings you here?" He said with a questioning look at Marlene.

"My dearest Major, this is my friend Fräulein Kupfer and

she's got herself into some trouble through no fault of her own," Bruni explained, batting her eyelashes.

"Hmm.. what kind of trouble exactly?" He gave Marlene the once-over, making her skin crawl.

"A terrible misunderstanding, *dorogoi*. My friend has such a good heart, she couldn't say no when she was coaxed into the student board several months ago. But as soon as she heard of the disrespectful things planned, she immediately wrote her resignation last week, because she doesn't want to have any part in any activities disrespecting our Soviet friends and benefactors."

Marlene watched the two of them with eagle eyes. The major didn't seem convinced, but he obviously was no match for the cunning Bruni.

"Look at her, Anatoly. Does she look like a troublemaker to you?" Bruni said and Marlene mustered her most innocent smile.

"I know about the awful happenings," he said, leaving it unclear whether he meant the demands of the students or the abductions last night. "It won't be easy to clear her name. There will be a lot of red tape involved." He looked expectantly at Bruni and shook his head with a sad expression. "And right now, where my mother is so sick…"

Bruni picked up on his demand instantly, leaving Marlene gawking at the well-rehearsed performance unfolding in front of her.

"Your poor mother! How could I forget, Anatoly? You're taking such great care of her, all the while being thousands of miles away here in Berlin." Bruni produced a small brown-paper bag from her handbag and laid it on his desk. "After hearing about her latest bout of sickness, I arranged for this."

He peeked into the bag, his eyes springing open. The bag disappeared into his uniform pocket faster than a lightning flash. Then he took up the phone and barked orders in Russian into the headset. When he returned his gaze to Bruni, he looked very satisfied. "Dearest Fräulein von Sinnen, your friend should be exonerated. But could you leave a copy of her resignation letter with me, just in case?"

"Certainly, dear Major Dengin." Bruni gave him a charming smile, retrieved the letter she and Marlene had prepared earlier, and handed it over to him. "Anything else you might need?"

"If I do, I'll come and see you at the club," he said, folding his thick fingers across his considerable stomach. Then the huge imposing man got up, his medals clinking as he walked them to the door. Marlene thought she would faint before she got out of the building and Bruni linked her arm to steady her.

"I'm going to look like death warmed over tonight after missing my beauty sleep," Bruni complained.

"I'm sorry," Marlene said. "I'm so grateful for all..."

"That's what friends are for," Bruni laughed. "Just stay out of trouble for a while. Not that I anticipate trouble after the major has sorted things out, but one can never be too careful."

That night Marlene was plagued with nightmares, expecting a knock on the door at any moment, but none came. In the morning she felt like she'd been run over by a tank and dragged herself to university, where everything went on as if nothing had happened. Nobody even whispered about the ghastly events from two nights ago, but Marlene felt as if the empty spaces of the taken students stared at her, accusing her of cowardice and betrayal.

After class, Lotte sidled up to her with a surprised look. "You here?"

"I can't stop my life, just because of this," Marlene said and then recounted what Bruni had done for her.

"But aren't you afraid?" Lotte closed her oversized shoulder bag, ready to return home.

"I'm terrified. Last night I barely closed an eye, afraid of hearing a knock on the door." Even in the streaming sunlight, Marlene felt the ice clog in her veins as images of NKVD police dragging her away stormed her brain.

"Can't you move out of the Soviet sector, at least for a while?" Lotte asked, bringing her back to the present.

It was a tempting idea. Because if she was horrified in plain daylight, how much worse would it be each night? And for how long? She shook her head. "I don't have any place to go…"

Lotte grinned at her with that cheeky smile only Lotte could pull off and said, "Move in with me."

"With you? What about your sisters?"

"Ursula just moved out after marrying Tom, and Anna and her family won't mind." Lotte looked at her and added, "And we sure could need someone to share the rent now that Ursula isn't here anymore."

Marlene laughed. Even before considering her parents' reaction, she decided the lure of feeling safe at night was too much to resist. "Okay, then."

Lotte hugged her, jumping up and down. "Let's go and get your things right now."

"Are you afraid I'll change my mind?"

"One can never be too sure," Lotte said and Marlene nodded.

CHAPTER 28

W hile it didn't come as a huge surprise, when the call came to summon him to the SMAD in Karlshorst Werner was visibly shaken.

As the vehicle stopped in front of the building, he stepped out with trepidation. Werner had been here many times and always found the building impressive, but today it looked dark and threatening. He suppressed a shudder and walked inside, where he was told to wait.

Several minutes later, a soldier came and said, "General Sokolov is ready to see you."

Sokolov sat at his monumental desk, looking down the table with six chairs in front of him. Five chairs were already occupied: chief-of-police Markgraf, SED head Gentner, two men from the NKVD and Kurt Lang, Werner's successor at the education department.

An acute awareness took hold of Werner and he felt his pulse ratcheting up. The setup promised a rather unpleasant meeting.

Sokolov cut right to the chase: "I must congratulate Comrades Markgraf, Gentner and Lang for the efficient and swift handling of a problem that might have been blown out of proportion had we let these misguided students continue on their path."

Werner's breath stuck in his lungs and he dared not breathe. His name hadn't been mentioned. That was a bad sign, and he could already hear the rattling wheels of the train destined for banishment.

After some more compliments, Sokolov turned toward Werner. "You may wonder why I invited Comrade Böhm to join our meeting."

The tightening noose around Werner's neck fell from his shoulders. If the general still called him *comrade*, he hadn't fallen from grace – yet.

"There's a taint to the entire action, because we couldn't get hold of one woman." Sokolov's alcoholic-red face turned into a deep purple.

Markgraf visibly flinched and promptly stood up. "Comrade Sokolov, our police arrived at her house as planned, but she wasn't there."

"I know that already! Tell me something I don't know!" Sokolov yelled, his expression turning into a pained grimace.

His ulcers are tormenting him again. Now he'll chew our asses until we feel the same pain he does, Werner thought.

"Yes, General, of course." Markgraf looked like he'd throw himself to the floor and literally lick Sokolov's boots. "We have immediately investigated the whereabouts of this woman. She was seen leaving the French sector in the morning, where she'd spent the night in a hotel with a French private called Etoile."

"Was the man questioned?" Sokolov asked, his stare furious and his voice intimidating.

Werner instinctively ducked, even though he wasn't on the receiving end of the general's wrath.

"Comrade General, we…the German police are not allowed to question Allied personnel," Markgraf replied, his limbs shaking.

Werner glanced at Norbert, somehow expecting him to come to Markgraf's help, but the other man didn't even blink. A sudden anger rose in Werner – the whole raid had been Norbert's idea, but now he let Markgraf pay for it. Bootlicking, cruel, power-craving sycophant Markgraf certainly deserved it, but somehow Werner was still annoyed at Norbert's betrayal.

It showed him very clearly his own position in this political game. Despite being a high-ranking SED official, he was nothing more than a dispensable pawn. One wrong step and he'd be taken off the playing field and tossed aside.

Markgraf continued talking: "…If you wanted to investigate the Frenchman, you'd have to file a formal request with the Kommandatura or wait until he enters the Russian sector and then your people could…"

"Stop! Useless louts! Why is it that I have to do everything myself to get it properly done?" Sokolov raged.

It was a rhetorical question, but the police chief nevertheless answered it: "Because we can't compete with your unmatched wisdom and foresight."

Werner wanted to retch on his shoes – or better yet on Sokolov's, for Markgraf to lick them clean again.

One of the NKVD sitting nearest to Sokolov whispered something into Sokolov's ear, and he wrinkled his brow, but then turned his attention to Markgraf again. "Comrade Markgraf, we'll leave the matter for the time being."

Werner's knees almost gave out with relief, but he'd rejoiced too soon.

"What do you think, Comrade Böhm? I believe you know that woman very well," Sokolov said suddenly.

All the blood drained from Werner's face. Had the entire conversation been set up in advance, meant to give him a false sense of security? What did they know? And what did they expect him to admit to?

He opted to play for time, admit only what they knew anyway.

"Yes, Comrade General, I remember her. She was on the student board, but always kept in the background, rarely said a word. I never identified her as a political agitator, unlike some of the other students."

"You've been seen with her quite frequently," the second NKVD officer said.

Cold sweat broke out on Werner's palms, but he resisted the urge to wipe them on his pants. That would give away his nerves. And an innocent man had no reason to be nervous. He forced himself to think quickly.

"Comrade, you are right. I met with her in private a couple of times, because I had the impression she had a soft spot for socialist ideas when not in the company of these agitators. It was my intention to convince her to join the SED."

"And did you?" Markgraf scoffed, a sly smirk on his face, and his waxed moustache twitching in merriment.

Werner wondered if he'd been under surveillance all this time. Had they somehow divined his carefully hidden criticism of Stalinism? Was this his final chance to stay in the party lane?

"I believe I did. The last time I saw her she was enthusiastic and eagerly asked me about the party office nearest where she lives." Werner looked from one man to the next, thinking how to maneuver himself – and Marlene – out of this corner. "But I'm afraid the unfortunate happenings might have scared her. She's not a very brave or strong woman." It hurt to say these words, but it was for the best, should they believe she was some easily intimidated girl.

Sokolov made a sharp movement with his hand. "I don't care either way. We got the ringleaders, and as soon as we have their confessions, this incident will never be mentioned again. She's not important for us or for the cause."

CHAPTER 29

Two days later all but three of the arrested students were released. They were badly roughed up, and so traumatized by their experience in Russian captivity that they immediately resigned their positions as student leaders and joined the SED.

"Please tell me about Georg and Julian – why haven't they been released? What has happened to them?" Marlene asked her fellow students.

"I have no idea," was the standard reply. She could see that they were terrified and refused to discuss the matter further.

"You should stop asking questions," one of them advised her. "The Soviets will stop at nothing to get what they want. I, for my part, want my family safe and alive."

Marlene's shoulders slumped. She felt like an awful coward to abandon Georg. Deep-rooted guilt prevented her from attending class today, so she skipped and went into town instead. She wandered around the streets. Most still showed the destruction of war, while some – mostly administrative buildings – had been slowly rebuilt. But while the

194

Berliners were willing to knuckle down and work, there was never enough money or materials to repair all the things needed.

The Soviets diverted most everything needed, including coal and steel from the Ruhr area, to Russia, letting the industry bleed out more every day. Supposedly the Western Allies had put a halt to the blatant robbery called reparations, at least in their zones, but oftentimes train wagons sent to Poland with agreed-upon reparation materials never returned, and continued eastward with or without their valuable freight.

Understandably the British, to whom the Ruhr area belonged, refused to send more coal if the train cars weren't returned first, and thus the Soviets staged a propaganda war on radio about the thieving and lying imperialists and stopped material going into Berlin in revenge. Living on an island amidst Soviet territory truly was a position between a rock and a hard place.

Marlene was so deep in thought that she didn't notice the car speeding down the street and would have walked under its wheels, if it weren't for someone holding her arm.

"Are you weary of life?" a familiar voice scolded her.

She turned around, spitting with madness. "You! Get the hell out of my way!"

Werner's face took on a hurt expression, and he pursed his lips as he said, "Shouldn't you rather thank me for saving your life?"

"Are you spying on me?"

"No, I'm not, I was on my way to the university. But despite your obvious hate for me, I couldn't very well let you walk under a car." Werner looked worried, haunted even, and she wondered whether he felt the increasing tension as well. But that wasn't her problem anymore, he himself had asked her never to talk to him again.

"Don't make it a habit to save my life," she said in the most scathing tone possible.

"Please, Marlene, can we talk for a moment?" he begged her.

She couldn't resist the trustful expression in his eyes. As much as she wanted to despise him, there was no way she could follow through with her plan. She nodded and followed him into a nearby bakery, where he ordered coffee for both of them.

"Forgive me, but it was the only way to…" He stopped mid-sentence, and gave her a vague smile. "Understand my situation – I was so overwhelmed by my emotions that I panicked. I've been a bachelor for such a long time, I got scared. But I never meant to hurt you…" She sensed he was lying, was making up an excuse to protect her. She needed to know the truth.

"Did you know about the raid that night?" she asked.

Werner flinched. "This kind of action isn't divulged to people outside the police department, and I'm not even involved with the university anymore."

Her blood boiled at the half-hearted attempted to deny his knowledge and before she could stop herself, she hissed, "You are a despicable coward, a beast. Be a man and at least admit your involvement. And stop defending the communist terror."

"All I ever wanted was to protect you, Marlene," he persisted.

"Why me? Why not all the others? Do you think they deserved to be roughed up by the people's police?" Marlene could barely keep herself from shouting.

His face fell. "I tried to warn them. You can't imagine how often I urged Georg to stop antagonizing the administration."

"The Soviet puppets, you mean?" She emptied the coffee cup, her hands trembling with barely suppressed fury.

"Let's not get into semantics. You know full well that I'm on your side, but there are greater powers that neither I nor anyone else can influence. The student board didn't heed my warnings." Werner rubbed his hands, seemingly unsure how to continue. "When people violate the rules, they have to bear the consequences for their actions. This is an omnipresent principle of any state structure."

"How can you still defend the communists? They're worse than the Nazis." She knew she should keep her mouth shut, but his slick, two-faced behavior irked her no end.

"If you believe that then I'm afraid you have a lot to learn," Werner said with a shrug. "At least thank the Soviet army for ridding Germany of the Nazis and bringing peace and stability to this country."

"I'll thank these communist thugs, rapists and murderers for nothing and I'll be the first one to cheer when they leave Berlin for good," she said in disgust. "And you know what? You're enabling the Soviet death grip on my city and therefore I hate you!"

For a moment he looked truly sad, but then he schooled his features again and answered, "I guess you should. I'm not worth your attention."

CHAPTER 30

Werner left the bakery in a very sour mood. Marlene had called him a despicable beast and a coward, but that wasn't the worst. What really got to him was that she was right. In a dozen years in the Soviet Union he'd learned to always toe the party line, never utter an independent or – God forbid – critical thought.

He'd looked away when his parents had fallen victim to the purge, had defended Stalin's regime when some of his best friends ended up in gulags for minor transgressions, had empathized with veterans of the Spanish Civil War and Lenin's comrades in arms who'd fallen in disgrace with Stalin.

He sighed. It wasn't something he was especially proud of, but sometimes the greater good required sacrifices. Individual hardships were inevitable during the transitional period until a truly socialist community was formed. The student board leaders' fates were such individual ones that couldn't be avoided, because their agitation might otherwise threaten the entire reform process of the German population.

The next morning, he got up in a much better mood and

looked out of the window. The day looked promising, with the sun shining resolutely through the cloudy sky. He hoped it wouldn't rain, since he hated the rain that made everything damp and filled the roads with puddles that were deceptive to drive through.

He arrived at his office in the *Haus der Einheit*, and sat down to work. Around noon, a knock on the door tore him from his concentration. "Come in!"

A uniformed Russian entered the room. "Comrade Böhm?"

"Yes, how can I help you?"

"General Sokolov expects you in Karlshorst. I'm here to drive you there," the man said briskly.

Werner sat in stunned silence for a moment, until the gravity of the order finally registered. A summons from the general was quite unexpected. It also augured unpleasantness, and with a sense of foreboding, Werner wondered what was in store for him.

"Certainly," he said and got up to grab his hat and coat before he followed the Russian to the black car waiting outside. Just when they left the building, the rain came pouring down. The wipers frantically waved backwards and forwards and still couldn't keep the windscreen clear.

Werner peered through the clouded glass, happy it wasn't him at the steering wheel trying to stay on the road, which was flooded by the sudden deluge. Inching along, and hitting every pothole, Werner finally arrived at the headquarters to meet his fate.

Throughout the journey he resisted the urge to try and ask the Russian about the reason for his summons. He wouldn't know anyway. At last the car stopped in front of the impressive SMAD headquarters. Long used to not being told what was going on, his mind still was in turmoil and his heart pounded.

It seemed the delegation had been waiting exclusively for

him, because the moment the car stopped, the doors opened and Paul Markgraf and an NKVD officer squeezed into the backseat.

"Comrade Böhm," the police chief greeted him.

The tiniest sigh escaped Werner's throat. As long as they still called him comrade, things couldn't be that bad. Despite knowing better, he asked, "Where are we going, Comrade Markgraf?"

"You'll see when we get there." Paul Markgraf guffawed and began complaining about the awful rain. Since weather was an innocuous topic, Werner joined the rant, although he carefully interspersed hidden praise about how much better he liked the weather in Moscow than in Berlin. The NKVD officer never said a single word, but Werner was sure he understood German quite well.

After about an hour's drive, the car stopped. As Werner got out, he noticed that a column of four cars, including theirs, had arrived. From one of them stepped General Sokolov himself, accompanied by his deputy and Norbert.

Werner respectfully gestured a greeting in their direction, but nobody acknowledged him. The grey bunker-like building turned out to be a former Gestapo prison, appropriated by the NKVD, who now used it for the same sinister acts as the previous owner, simply changing the underlying ideology.

He'd never been inside such an installation, but had heard the gleefully reported details about the atrocities Hitler's cronies had committed, along with whispered rumors about similar things happening to those unfortunate souls in NKVD custody. His legs suddenly felt like jelly as he stepped into the concrete monolith.

They walked through a labyrinth of passages until they came to a large brightly lit chamber filled with all manner of implements designed to elicit a confession from a suspect. Werner noticed a man with his hands cuffed behind his back and hooked to a chain that suspended him from the ceiling. When the man's head swung around, he recognized it was Georg.

Werner gasped in shock. He had never in his life seen a more repulsive sight. The bile rose in his throat and he fought it down. *Why did they bring me here?* He wished to flee from the room and scream his horror to the world. But he could do no such thing. Marlene's face appeared in front of his inner eye and her verdict about him echoed through his mind. *Coward! Beast! Monster!* Intuitively he ducked, awaiting her slap his face.

"No stomach for this business, eh, Werner? We'll have to toughen you up," Markgraf said, before he beckoned him to come outside. Werner was never more thankful for an order.

General Sokolov was standing outside smoking. Werner almost stumbled with shock when the general addressed him directly, "Comrade Böhm. You may wonder why you're here."

"Yes, Comrade General."

"The reason is, Comrade Gentner has informed me that you had befriended Georg Tauber," Sokolov said casually.

Werner's heart missed a beat. There it was. He would be punished for the crime of being friends with a dissenter. He hurried to explain, "Comrade General, I befriended this criminal subject on orders from—"

Sokolov cut him off with a move of his hand. "I know. I know. Among all the students we interrogated there's only these two, Georg Tauber and Julian Berger, who refuse to confess their crimes. We really would like to close this unfortunate chapter and move on to more important things. But, we need a confession, and a public recantation of their outrageous claims. And this is where you come into play. Talk some sense

201

into them, appeal to their reason, bribe them, do whatever you want, but make them sign a recantation."

"Yes, Comrade General," Werner said, wondering how on earth he was supposed to achieve what the NKVD henchmen hadn't. Did Sokolov truly believe a few sweet words could change the mind of a person who had withstood days of torture?

His stomach a nervous wreck, Werner entered the interrogation room again. Gratefully he realized that the tormenters had left and he was alone with Georg. He approached the young man, who looked as if he were asleep.

"Georg," he said, waiting until the other man half-opened a heavily swollen eye. "It's me, Werner."

"You?" was all the other man said.

"I'm so sorry, I had no idea," Werner said, more to himself than to Georg. He knew they were being watched through the one-way viewing pane on the wall, so he chose his words with care. "They brought me here to talk some sense into you. Please, you must confess to the accusations and recant your demands if you want to get out of here."

"Never," Georg croaked.

"Please. Save yourself, and your family. I promise you'll leave this room a free man today, but you have to confess. Don't make this any worse than it already is," Werner begged the courageous man, while he secretly loathed himself for being such a weakling, condoning these barbaric acts through his behavior.

Suddenly he felt like he'd lost his last morsel of humanity. He'd become a monster, equally despicable as the torturers listening outside.

"Spare your words. I will never recant the truth and my fight for freedom. I have survived three years in a Nazi camp – I sure as hell won't succumb to the rotten communists," Georg spat out. The speech had used up all his energy and his chin slumped onto his chest.

Werner couldn't stand to witness how his former friend was digging his own grave, and tried once more. In a hushed voice he suggested, "You don't have to give up your beliefs. Just tell them what they want to hear so that they set you free. Think of your family, too. Do you think they will be spared if you continue to challenge the system?"

"You may not understand, but unlike you, I will never sell my soul. Now leave me alone!" Georg closed his eyes and turned his head away.

Werner stepped out of the room to reunite with the Soviet officers and Markgraf. "I'm sorry, there's nothing I can do. This man stubbornly refuses to see reason in a misguided effort to protect his criminal beliefs."

General Sokolov balled his hands into fists and yelled several Russian curses before he ordered his men, "There's nothing left for us to do here. Hold a trial, sentence them to twenty-five years of hard labor for espionage and malicious propaganda against the Soviet population and its institutions. And you," he turned toward Werner, "come with me."

Werner's knees trembled violently but he somehow managed to follow the general into another room, where he was handed paper and a pen.

"Write a confession and recant all defamatory claims in the name of these two criminals," Sokolov instructed him.

It took him a few moments to actually comprehend what he was being asked to do. Numb with fear and self-loathing, he sat down and wrote a glowing confession that would hold up under the strongest scrutiny by any political officer. When he was finished, he handed two sheets of paper to an NKVD officer, one for Georg and one for Julian. The officer assured him that he would take care of the rest, falsifying signatures to the statements, and dismissed him.

Werner boarded the car and returned to Berlin, thoroughly disgusted with himself. Georg was right, he was a sorry excuse for a human being. Shame washed over him, remembering that Georg's spirit remained unbroken while his own was shattered.

CHAPTER 31

Marlene and Lotte returned home after classes and found Zara sitting on their doorstep, waiting for them. Her hair was tousled and her cheeks were flushed with agitation.

"What's the matter?" Marlene asked her.

"Nothing," Zara said, but taking a single look into her fright-filled eyes, Marlene knew there was a whole lot of nothing going on.

"Come in, and I'll make us tea," Lotte offered.

Once the three of them were sitting around the kitchen table with a cup of tea in their hands, Marlene finally coaxed Zara into telling them the reason for her distress. She'd been harassed by Russian soldiers when leaving the restaurant where she worked in the French sector.

"Thankfully, a couple of French soldiers heard my screams and intervened," Zara said miserably. "If I'm not safe in the Western sectors, where else will I be safe from these beasts?"

"Not in Berlin," Lotte said, and both her friends stared at her.

"Are you saying Zara should move to West Germany?" Marlene asked in disbelief.

"There she would be safe from the Russians, as they can't go walking around in the other zones." Lotte took another sip from her cup.

"But how? It's not like people can just move around as they please," Zara sighed. "I would need a permit, and a job. I don't even know anyone outside Berlin."

"I can ask around," Lotte offered. "My sister works for the American hospital and she has quite a few friends there."

Once again Marlene was grateful that she had moved out of the Soviet sector after that fateful night. The notion of what could have happened to her still sent shudders of angst deep into her soul. Even though she was still angry at Werner for breaking her heart, she secretly thanked him for rescuing her and wished she could one day see him again under different circumstances.

But so far it didn't look as if politics would ever leave her life. Maybe she should consider moving to the Western zone as well? But the next moment she shivered at the idea. Berlin was her home, she'd never lived anywhere else and she couldn't fathom leaving the city she loved so much.

Putting on blinders and keeping her head down was the best way to weather the current tension. She and the other Germans were only pawns in the game about their own future.

Several days later she and Lotte were listening to the Soviet-controlled Radio Berlin, and she dropped the cup filled with tea when the radio speaker announced an important news program with the newly appointed radio chief editor Werner Böhm.

The hot liquid spilled across the kitchen table and dripped to the floor, despite Lotte's efforts to contain the damage.

Marlene herself sat frozen in place, enrapt by Werner's sonorous voice as he announced, "In the matter of the illegal and radical protests by some students against the well-being of the working population, the two main perpetrators Georg Tauber and Julian Berger have confessed their crimes and recanted the hateful imperialist propaganda they have spewed."

Marlene glued her ears to the radio, Werner's image appearing in her mind, and she listened full of horror as he read first Julian's and then Georg's confession.

"That can't be true!" she yelled. "Georg would never say such a thing."

Lotte put a hand on her arm, trying to calm her down. "Maybe he did it to save himself or his family. You know what the others have said…"

"No, no, no…" Marlene slumped onto the table, her head resting on her forearm, and she barely heard the conclusion of Werner's speech.

"…these two parasites upon the people have no place in our democratic state and according to their heinous crimes they have been sentenced to twenty-five years of hard labor."

"No!" she yelled with all her strength and jumped up from the table, ready to storm out of the apartment and take on the world.

Lotte stepped into her path and said, "You need to calm down. There's nothing you can do. Or do you want to join them in Siberia?"

Marlene slumped back on her chair, disillusioned by the world. "I'm not going back. I'm dropping out," she muttered.

"Don't be irrational, you can't give up now." Lotte poured her some more tea.

"Irrational? Me? The Russian thugs are irrational! I'll never set foot into that wretched place again," Marlene said bitterly.

"If you give up, then the Russians win," Lotte replied. "They don't care if you stay or quit. You make no difference to them. The only person you will be hurting by stopping your studies is yourself."

"I know you're right, but how can I carry on as if nothing has happened? Oh, God, there has to be something I can do to help Georg and Julian." Marlene held her head in her hands as if it was going to burst.

"Maybe there's nothing but keep studying, so one day we become lawyers and may help others unjustly arrested." Lotte looked as desperate as Marlene felt. They sat for a few moments in silence before Lotte said, "You know what? Let's go shopping!"

"Shopping?" Marlene looked at her friend in stunned amazement, certain the other woman had completely lost her mind. Almost two years after the war there was rarely anything to be found on the shelves, except for food and the most basic necessities of life.

"Yes. Let's go to the black market." Lotte broke out into a huge grin, already anticipating the joys of window-shopping at the area around Tiergarten in the British sector.

Marlene of course knew that the black market existed and that desperate Germans disposed of everything not in immediate need, like fine clothing, jewelry, silverware, paintings and children's toys. Buyers were mostly the Allied soldiers, or those who worked for them, but in addition army-issue goods like watches, clothes and rations could be found, discreetly sold by those in the business of bartering between occupiers and occupied.

Out of fear of being caught, Marlene had never been there herself. It was well known that the British frequently raided the market but could never really shut it down. Rumors had it that they once picked up a Russian general engaged in illicit trading, but the Allied personnel were never sent to prison for such a crime, unlike the Germans doing the same.

Maybe the thrill of visiting the forbidden market would take her mind off Georg's awful fate.

"Okay, let's go," Marlene said, and she grabbed her hat and coat.

CHAPTER 32

W erner left the radio station after the program where he condemned the two young men and read the fake confessions he'd been forced to write himself.

Disgusted was too benign a word for what he felt. While he hadn't tortured the men himself, he'd been the willing tool of those who couldn't defend socialism without resorting to violence. He hunched his shoulders forward, the gnawing pain in his stomach becoming more forceful every day.

Politische Bauchschmerzen, political stomachache it was called among those people who still believed one should put country over party and not the other way round. He scoffed. The situation was long beyond the question of party or country and had come down to human decency.

Julian and Georg were good men, not the heinous traitors they were painted. Both of them had resisted the Nazis, the same way they now resisted the Soviet oppression. And the so-called communists treated them the same way the Nazis had done: sending the men to a concentration camp.

Georg could have thrown Werner under the bus by

revealing his part in the American shooting of the Russian soldiers who tried to rape the German girl, but even under extreme torture he never did. Werner admired and envied the upstanding character of the young man who chose torture and death rather than undermining his integrity.

He did not recognize the theories of Marx and Lenin anymore. These great thinkers had always striven for a better, more just world for the oppressed workers and farmers. But Stalin had perverted the communist ideal and transformed it into a tool of terror, inequality and unlawfulness. Every single critical thought could result in arrest, incarceration or even death.

With sudden clarity of mind, he realized that Stalinism was exactly what George Orwell had written about in his book *Animal Farm*, published two years earlier. The critical book, although it never mentioned the Soviet Union or Stalin, had been put on the index of forbidden books in the Soviet zone the moment it was first published, but here in Berlin, Werner had been able to find a copy in a British library.

Dominion of the swine, how fitting. And I must be one of the cruel and merciless dogs, keeping the other animals at bay. A painful ache drilled through his heart. Marlene had called him a beast who sold his soul to the devil.

He couldn't continue to live with blood on his hands, couldn't continue to be a Russian stooge.

He just couldn't.

But what should he do?

For the next few weeks he went through his daily tasks like an automaton. He didn't find joy in anything anymore, always afraid of the consequences of his actions. A thousand times he pondered telling someone about his political stomachaches, but never uttered more than a few carefully disguised insinuations.

He knew there must be likeminded independent thinkers, but all of them carefully withheld their true feelings, just like he did.

One day he visited Norbert on a social occasion and used the opportunity to address his concerns.

"Don't you think the German people should be able to experience the merits of the communist ideology without force? I mean, wouldn't that endear us more to them?" he asked.

Norbert raised an eyebrow, as if deeply worried. "Those are the words of a very naïve person. You really should know better by now."

Werner knew he should shut up, but he tried again. "I'm just concerned. For some strange reasons the Berliners preferred to vote for the imperialists last December. And since then the anti-Soviet mood has only augmented. What will happen in another election? Aren't you afraid they will wipe us out completely?"

"We're taking precautions already," Norbert said. "There will never be a lost election for the SED again. You'd better forget your qualms and arrive in the real world." And then he added with a warning undertone, "You wouldn't want to risk your career by saying something foolish."

"Not at all." Werner instinctively stood taller, demonstrating to the First Secretary of the SED that he didn't have any dissenting ideas. He had maneuvered himself into a corner with no way out except into a gulag.

Several days later he attended an official event, to celebrate the second anniversary of the German capitulation, in the SMAD headquarters in Karlshorst. The huge ballroom with the five-yard-high ceiling was decorated with the flags of the four occupying powers, and long rows of tables with dark green tablecloths were set with the finest china and crystal glassware for a formidable state banquet.

The host, General Sokolov, had spared neither trouble nor expense to dish up the most exquisite delicacies for the guests from the other Allied powers. Crimean champagne, caviar, borscht, solyanka, pirozhki, pelmeni, and beef stroganoff were just a few of the prepared dishes.

Throughout the six-course dinner, glorious speech after glorious speech was given by Soviet dignitaries, praising how the Red Army had single-handedly won World War Two and liberated Europe from the Nazi yoke.

Werner thought it was disrespectful to the Western Allies who'd also done their share to win against the Nazis, but didn't even get an honorable mention in the speeches. His gaze fell on the American Kommandant Dean Harris, recently promoted to Brigadier General, and he observed how much Harris had to control himself to grin and bear it.

At long last, General Sokolov got up to speak, extolling the virtues of Mother Russia and her brave men. His fabrications went on and on, punctuated by fervent applause from his men and polite hand-clapping from the other Allies. But Werner wasn't fooled. He saw the disdain on the faces of every French, British, and American man in the room when Sokolov droned on about the good that the Soviet Union had done in Berlin.

For obvious reasons he failed to mention how the city was robbed to pay for war reparations, while he stressed the egregious ingratitude of the Germans who couldn't seem to understand the virtues of communism.

After the dinner, Werner mingled with the other attendees, always careful not to seem too friendly with the foreigners and never praising anything they did or said. He listened in on a discussion between Harris and Sokolov and found the American Kommandant incredibly kind and patient, even in the face of the vile accusations the Russian made.

Werner remembered when those parties radiated the spirit of unity instead of the current suspicion and disdain against the other side. Only two years earlier, everyone had looked brightly into the future, while now the two systems faced each other as implacable enemies.

But what struck him during this banquet was that most of the spite, intransigence and stubborn insistence on their opinion came from the Soviet side, while the Americans weren't the monsters the propaganda painted them.

He returned home way past midnight, but he couldn't sleep all night, because of the whirling thoughts in his head. In the wee hours of the morning he undertook a momentous decision. Giddy with excited determination he got up long before his Russian superiors woke up and took the public transport to visit Dean Harris in his office.

CHAPTER 33

Bruni's smile was even more dazzling than usual. The Café de Paris had arranged – with the help of a few admirers – a surprise party for its star. The place teemed with French, British and American soldiers and their German Fräuleins.

Marlene felt small and insignificant as she congratulated her friend, who looked stunning in yet another iridescent gown with matching high heels.

"Happy birthday, Bruni." Marlene hugged her.

"Thanks so much for coming." Bruni grinned from ear to ear. "Isn't this such a wonderful surprise?"

"It truly is," Zara said, and then took her turn in hugging the birthday girl.

Lotte had been invited too and observed the plush setting with wide eyes. She whispered in Marlene's ear, "I had no idea these things still existed in Berlin."

Marlene nodded. She'd grown used to the two-tiered society, with Allied soldiers bathing in luxuries while the German population barely scraped by. It was the price they had to pay for Hitler's delusions of grandeur. But the party today was different from the previous times she'd attended the Café de Paris.

It took her a while before she found the reason. No Russians were present. Given Bruni's history of being on the best terms with all the occupiers, this was a clear sign that the publicly shown unity between the four powers was fragile at best.

Marlene wondered what the future held in store for her city, if the Allied Kommandatura was too disunited to make the required unanimous decisions. Would they hand over the decision-making to the Germans? Or would they rather agree to give the entire city to the Soviet Union in exchange for regions near the inner-German border? She shuddered at the thought of Berlin becoming part of the Soviet-occupied zone.

Despite having sworn to forget Werner, she automatically thought about him and what he might be doing right now. Then she shrugged. She had once believed him a fine, considerate man, and she had cared for him deeply. But after his latest radio broadcast reading the confessions, which she knew in her heart couldn't be true, she'd lost every vestige of respect for him – a spineless weasel only interested in himself and his career. Should he do whatever he wanted, it wasn't her concern anymore.

People began chanting for Bruni to sing. She graciously – and proudly – obliged and took her place on the stage. Dean Harris held a short speech after her song, and then drinks flowed and waitresses entered carrying trays of hors d'oeuvres, offering the guests the bite-sized delicacies. It was a boisterous atmosphere, just like it had been before the war. Marlene herself had been too young back then, but she knew from stories of older people and from motion pictures about the Roaring Twenties what it had been like in cosmopolitan Berlin.

Loud music filled the air and interrupted her musings. A

216

handsome American GI suddenly stood in front of her and asked her to dance with him. She couldn't very well deny him. After all, she'd come to have fun and forget about the misery for a while.

The GI proved to be a good dancer and despite her secret yearning for Werner, she enjoyed herself very much. Shortly before midnight, she saw Bruni and Dean Harris sneak out and leave the inebriated guests to themselves. Marlene took it as her cue to search for Lotte, who'd been whisked away by a British soldier.

"Hey, Lotte, I'm about to go home. You want to come with me?"

"Sure." Lotte seemed thankful for Marlene's interruption and whispered in her ear, "It's high time for me to leave. My admirer is getting a bit handsy."

Marlene nodded knowingly. Lotte was still waiting for her fiancé to return from Russian captivity and while she was outgoing and fun, she never enjoyed more than a harmless flirtation. Together they scanned the room for Zara, who was in a deep embrace with a handsome man.

"You want to leave with us?" Marlene asked, but the soft flush on Zara's cheeks told her the answer, even before the other woman shook her head.

CHAPTER 34

Dean was in a bad mood. Due to the Soviets' veto the new Lord Mayor Ernst Reuter still couldn't take office. The elections had taken place several months ago already and nothing had changed, because the Soviets filibustered, obstructed and asked for additional investigations.

And there was nothing he could do. General Clay, his superior in the Allied Control Council, had explicitly told him not to antagonize the Russians. As if those thugs needed antagonizing. They came up with the vilest shit all by themselves.

For the time being Dean was stuck with a Berlin Magistrat filled with unelected communist members, while the elected delegates were kept out of office with the flimsiest of excuses. How on earth was he supposed to govern Berlin under these circumstances?

A knock on the door interrupted his thoughts. He looked up in surprise. It was early in the morning and his men knew not to disturb him during the quiet hour before the official office hours began.

"Come in," he called.

The door opened slowly, almost reluctantly, and the man who peered inside wasn't in uniform. For a moment Dean considered sending him away, but then he recognized Werner Böhm. *Now, that's a surprise!*

He kind of liked Böhm, who – although a staunch communist – always tried to stick to facts and reason. The last time they'd had a short conversation was at the horrible two-year anniversary of the capitulation in Karlshorst. He wondered what the Moscow stooge could possibly want this early in the morning.

"Good morning, Herr Kommandant," Böhm said, standing in the doorframe, nervously scanning the room. He looked like he hadn't slept all night, with dark shadows beneath his alert eyes. "Do you have a minute to talk…in private?"

Dean was thoroughly intrigued and pointed to the chair in front of his desk. "Close the door and take a seat, please."

"Herr Kommandant," Böhm said in flawless English, "I have an unusual request, but first I must ask you for complete confidentiality. Nobody can know about our conversation."

Dean cocked his head. Things were getting stranger by the minute, and he wondered what kind of top-secret mission Böhm was on. Did he bring a peace offering from Sokolov on the matter of the Lord Mayor? Unlikely. The Soviets didn't send German communists to negotiate with the other Allies.

Or did Böhm know something about the four hundred abducted German engineers, whisked away to the Soviet Union during a cloak-and-dagger operation to work for their new masters? But why would he come to him? What did he want in return?

"Nobody will learn about this conversation from me," Dean said and leaned back, quietly observing how Böhm nodded and fidgeted with his hands while taking a seat. The man was supremely nervous. For a moment Dean feared the German might be planning something stupid, and felt for the pistol he always kept in the open drawer of his desk.

During his two years in Berlin he'd received countless anonymous death threats, but he'd never actually considered someone coming into his office to kill him. Germans weren't allowed to carry weapons, either. Not even the police. He relaxed again and shoved the frightening thought aside.

"This might sound rather strange to you, but..." Böhm inhaled deeply before he continued. "...I'm seeking your help to leave Berlin."

Dean was stunned into silence, while the wheels in his brain set in motion and connected the dots. After long moments of silence, he asked, "You want to defect?"

Böhm buried his face in his hands before he looked up again and responded, "Yes. I...I have witnessed such awful things that I simply cannot stay loyal to the Soviets anymore. And...I'm afraid they will find out about my critical opinion and make me disappear forever. I got to know you as an honorable and upright man, therefore I'm coming here laying my fate in your hands." Böhm bowed his head, as if waiting for Dean to sever his neck with a sharp blade.

Dean was speechless. Sure, there had been cases of defectors, mostly from the Soviet-occupied zone, but nobody as high up in the hierarchy as Böhm. He was a big fish – one that Dean could possibly exploit for anti-Soviet propaganda, maybe even use his intricate knowledge of the Soviet workings to coax Sokolov into agreeing to some of the disputed points at the Kommandatura. But...how could he know this wasn't a ploy? He decided to get more information first.

"You're right, that's quite an unusual request and you will forgive me for having to ask some questions first." The secret dossier he had on Böhm depicted the man as reasonable and humane, but a loyal Russian operative. Many defectors had become spies and Harris had to be careful, since such an incident might cause friction in both the Kommandatura and the Allied Control Council.

Böhm nodded. "Anything you want."

Dean couldn't help but smile at the other man, who was so obviously desperate. "You must know that there's no way back, ever. So, what made you take this decision?"

"I have come to the conclusion that Stalin and his cronies have perverted the idea of communism to such a point that I can't shoulder the responsibility of being part of these crimes against humanity." Böhm straightened his shoulders and his eyes locked with Dean's. "You will understand that I need to keep some of my knowledge as a pledge to make sure you get me safely out of Berlin and into the American zone in Germany. But I promise to tell your people everything I know, including…" Böhm looked around the room as if to make sure nobody was present to overhear them. "…the truth about the student leaders Tauber and Berger."

Dean suppressed a gasp. Böhm had just validated his suspicions about the sudden confessions of the student leaders who fought for more democracy and less indoctrination. But he thought it wiser not to react to the bait.

"I understand your need to keep an ace up your sleeve, but I will need something with more substance to believe you. Smuggling a man of your position out of Berlin isn't an easy undertaking and we risk the wrath of your Soviet masters."

Böhm visibly flinched when Dean mentioned his Soviet masters, which led him to believe Böhm was telling the truth. More than ever Dean wished to have one of his experienced interrogators by his side. But since he'd promised the other man absolute confidentiality, he had to rely on his own instincts.

"I can't divulge anything right now, because if I do, and the

221

Soviets somehow find out…" Böhm didn't finish his sentence. "Please, you must believe me. I will answer any and all questions as soon as I'm in a safe place." Böhm's pleading face shook Dean to the core. Having fought his way from Normandy all the way across the Rhine, he knew a desperate man when he saw one.

"All right. Walk from the Brandenburger Tor in the direction of Tiergarten at 8 a.m. tomorrow morning. Someone will ask you for directions to Alexanderplatz. Follow this person," he instructed Böhm, while his mind fervently tried to come up with a plan to take it from there. "Don't take anything with you, except for a briefcase with your most precious things."

Böhm nodded and made to get up.

"One more thing. If you're not alone or are followed, we scrub the entire operation, and there won't be a second chance," Dean said.

"Understood. And thank you." Böhm hesitated for a split second, but then turned around and left the room, leaving Dean frantically thinking about a way to get the defector out of Berlin.

By air, obviously, but how to get him safely to Tempelhof Airport? And whom should he send to the meeting point? It had to be a civilian, someone entirely innocuous. A woman.

He picked up the phone to dial the number of his deputy and organize Böhm's escape from the Soviet sphere of influence.

CHAPTER 35

July 1947

On his way home, Werner was plagued with doubts. For one thing, he didn't have anything but Dean Harris' word. What if the American turned on him and called Sokolov? Cold sweat broke out and ran in rivulets down his back.

He balled his trembling hands into fists and hid them in the pockets of his coat. He had no option but to trust Harris, since he'd gambled his life on the premise that an American promise had more substance than a Russian one. What if he had misjudged the American Kommandant?

Suddenly he began to see NKVD police at every corner, ready to pounce on him. Completely shaken and exhausted he arrived at his office in the *Haus der Einheit*.

"Hey, Böhm, running late today?"

His head snapped in the direction of the caller, instinctively raising his hands to parry an attack. "Oh, good morning, Comrade, the bus had to stop because of an accident."

The colleague shook his head. "I really don't understand why you insist on using public transport when your position comes with the availability of a driver."

"Because it gives me a glimpse into the minds of the Berliners, which is useful for my propaganda work," Werner said and hurried into his office, before he could give the other man a piece of his mind.

What was more non-communist than the political elites driving by car, while the highly praised workers had to use public transport? Didn't his colleagues notice the irony of it all? Didn't anybody question whether all these spoils and privileges were compatible with Marx's theories? The cars, the food, the *pajoks*, the villas, the trips to special recreation homes for party functionaries...the list went on and on.

Nobody expected Norbert Gentner to live in a rotten basement with twelve other comrades like the industrial workers had to, but did he have to reside in a twenty-five-room villa with an old stock of trees in Pankow?

Werner shrugged and settled at his desk to read the headlines of several newspapers, including the Soviet *Tägliche Rundschau*, the American *Neue Zeitung* and the British *Die Welt*.

The usual bickering. Nothing of substance. He turned to the correspondence on his desk and diligently worked through it until the phone rang. He stared at the black apparatus and then at the watch on his desk. Way past noon. He'd forgotten to go for lunch.

"Werner Böhm, SED headquarters, department for media and..."

"Comrade Böhm, you're requested at SMAD immediately," a Russian voice barked into the phone.

Hot and cold shivers attacked Werner and he stammered, "Yes, Comrade, I'll take a car this very instant and will arrive within the hour." The other person hung up, leaving Werner frozen into place with fright.

The only explanation for this was that Harris had broken his promise and alerted the Soviets. He pondered whether he should run, try to flee from Berlin on his own. But how, and where to? Or maybe it wasn't Harris who'd talked, but they'd been observing him and now wanted to find out the reason for his visit with the American Kommandant.

Werner clung to this notion like a lifeline. He would play for time, trust that the American hadn't sold him out. He had only twenty more hours to endure. Putting on a confident smile, he told his secretary that he was needed in Karlshorst and might not return in the afternoon.

Sweating like a decathlete, his nerves were strung tight as he arrived at Karlshorst, where he'd been not long before for the celebrations of the anniversary of Germany's unconditional surrender. What a different setting it had been back then.

Today the sentry looked grim and beckoned him to enter the huge ballroom. The room was crowded with mostly men in uniform and Werner gave a silent sigh of relief. They surely hadn't called half of the garrison just to expose him as a dissenter. He nodded at familiar faces and finally found Norbert in the crowd.

"Comrade Norbert, what's going on?" he asked his boss.

"An awful thing happened. Sokolov will speak in a few minutes," Gentner said.

When Sokolov climbed the podium twenty minutes later and told the crowd that France and Britain had had the guts to invite twenty-two European countries to the so-called Marshall Conference in Paris, Werner wanted to weep with joy.

"This is a direct affront against the first socialist state, the

Soviet Union, and all our brother countries in the world. The imperialist warmongers and enemies of the people are finally showing their real faces. They have succumbed to the American capitalists' intent of destroying the world and flung the gauntlet against the peace-loving people's democracies." Sokolov droned on and on about the perceived impudence of the Americans wanting to help war-ravaged Europe and even include the socialist Eastern European states. It was a vile plan for interference in the domestic affairs of other countries and showed once again the American quest for economic imperialism and domination.

Werner stopped listening. In reality, the Soviets objected to the Marshall Plan for more petty reasons. They didn't want to tolerate economic aid to Germany, because this nation had greatly devastated the Soviet Union just a few years earlier and should pay the price for decades to come.

When the British and French representatives wouldn't agree to the Soviet's demands of having complete control over any aid given to Germany plus the knowledge of which nation was given how much money by the Americans, the Soviet Foreign minister stormed out of the meeting. And now he was offended, that the other Allies pursued the plan without him?

Distortion of facts and fear-based reporting had become such an ingrained part of the Soviet-style communism that Werner wanted to puke. Any doubts whether it was the right thing to defect instead of trying to reform the system from within vanished not only with Sokolov's words, but also with the subsequent unanimous condemnation of the American effort to actually help starving people.

There was no way Werner could stand behind this cruel system one moment longer. He anxiously awaited the next morning when he'd leave all of this behind and start a new life.

After lengthy discussions and dinner, he didn't return to his office, but told the driver to take him directly to the apartment in Pankow he shared with Horst. Much to his relief, his roommate wasn't home, which gave him the time to say goodbye. He wandered through the apartment, impressing every detail upon his memory.

Then he packed his briefcase, taking only the most precious things with him – his identity documents, money, a picture of his parents, a small booklet his first politics teacher had given him back in Moscow.

His fingers caressed the heavy paperweight Marlene had given him. Memories of her saddened his soul. He'd never see her again, and he couldn't even take her gift with him. In case he was stopped and searched, he could only take things that wouldn't awaken suspicion.

With a weary heart he went to sleep, hoping he was making the correct decision. Because once he defected, he'd never be able to return. Not to Berlin, and not to the Soviet Union. He'd never see any of his friends – and his parents, should they still be alive – again. A single tear rolled down his cheek. He wiped it away. Then he wrote a letter to Marlene, hoping the Americans would be able to give it to her.

The next morning, he woke well before dawn, giddy with anticipation, but also full of fear. He took great care with getting dressed, shaved and combed and then left everything the same way as every other day. When his going missing would inevitably be noticed, they would think he'd left for the office and perhaps gotten involved in an accident.

He opened yesterday's *Pravda* newspaper to the page of an article about the successful land reform, as if he intended to continue reading after work and then left the apartment. Dawdling and taking extra precautions that nobody followed him, he arrived at the Brandenburg Gate two minutes early. As instructed, he followed the Charlottenburger Chaussee, which the Nazis had included in their megalomaniac project "World Capital Germania" and renamed East-West-Axis, into the direction of the S-Bahn Tiergarten station.

Purposely walking slowly, he soon saw a platinum-blonde woman stepping out from behind some trees lining the Chaussee, walking directly toward him. His heart missed a beat or two, while he pretended not to notice her.

"Excuse me, *mein Herr*, could you please tell me how to get to Alexanderplatz?" A melodious voice trilled.

He recognized the singer Brunhilde von Sinnen and wondered whether this was a coincidence or whether she actually worked for the Americans. But since no other person was nearby, he answered with fear gnawing at his stomach, "Certainly, Fräulein von Sinnen, I'll show you the way."

"Come with me," she said, linking her arm with his. She behaved as if they were on a romantic date and steered him toward the Tiergarten station. From there they took the train a few stations deep into the American sector and surfaced at the German Opera, where she waved down a taxi.

Fräulein von Sinnen told him to get inside before she turned around and left. His heart stopped. Now he was sure it was a trap. Hadn't she been Orlovski's paramour? Had the Russians promised her to return Feodor if she turned him in?

"Wait," he called after her and quickly fumbled the envelope with Marlene's name from his briefcase. "Can you please give this to your friend Fräulein Kupfer?"

She nodded and put the letter in her purse.

"Hop in. Fast," the driver said with a thick American accent and Werner did just that. He was handed an American army cap and told to put it on.

"So, this is my escape?" he asked the driver, who turned toward him with a broad grin.

"Looks like it. Seems the bosses really want you. We're going straight to Tempelhof."

Tempelhof, the American airport. They'd decided to fly him out right away. Werner knew it wasn't his to ask any more questions, so he contented himself with thanking the driver and watching the buildings fly by at breakneck speed.

With nothing else to occupy his mind he scrutinized his decision for the umpteenth time. Meeting with Fräulein von Sinnen had kindled his doubts. Would his defection validate Marlene's judgement of him as a spineless coward? Should he have stayed and fought? Could he have changed a thing?

They arrived at the Tempelhof airport and a sentry stopped the car to ask for their credentials. The driver showed his identity card and the man quickly waved them through, and they drove around the building directly onto the airfield.

Werner was impressed. The car stopped beside a plane already waiting on the field and he was relieved to recognize Dean Harris coming down the gangway.

"Welcome to American soil," he greeted him. ""You'll be flying with General Clay on his private plane to Wiesbaden Airport. He'll instruct you about the further procedure."

"Thank you so much, Herr Kommandant," Werner said and shook Harris' hand. "I'll be forever indebted to you."

Then he walked up the gangway to join General Clay, whom he'd seen on several formal occasions in the SMAD, but had never actually talked to. Within minutes they were airborne, and Werner soon found out that Clay wasn't the monster the Soviets painted him as, but was in fact an intelligent and friendly man.

CHAPTER 36

R IAS radio was playing music when a ringing sounded. Marlene and Lotte both looked up from their homework, confused by the unfamiliar sound.

"What was that?" Marlene asked.

"I think the doorbell – they finally repaired it yesterday. I'll go and have a look." Lotte got up and opened the door. Moments later she stood in the room with Bruni in tow.

"Bruni! What brings you here?" Marlene almost choked. Bruni rarely came to visit.

"I have a letter for you." Bruni smiled and produced an envelope with Marlene's name on it from her purse.

"Since when do you deliver the mail? Doesn't the Café de Paris pay you enough?" Marlene teased.

Bruni pursed her lips and held the letter between her red-painted fingers. "Instead of making snappish remarks you should fall on your knees and kiss my feet for bringing this to you."

Marlene squinted her eyes and recognized the handwriting on the envelope. "Oh, Bruni! Where did you get this?"

"This I can't tell and I'm sorry for the delay, but I had to wait a few days before giving it to you."

Marlene furrowed her brow. It wasn't at all like Bruni to play the mysterious one. She yanked the letter from her friend's hands, ripped it open and read what Werner had written.

My dearest Marlene,

You were right, I have been a despicable coward and many suffered because of my weakness, including you.

This is no excuse for my behavior, but if you knew the pressures I had to deal with, you might understand why I behaved as I did. In the end, you were the one who opened my eyes and showed me what it means to defend what you believe in.

I never meant to hurt you and my feelings for you were real. I spent that night with you to keep you out of your house, but I slept with you because I love you. My only regret is that I couldn't share the truth with you, and I hope you will forgive me one day. We may never meet again, but rest assured that my thoughts will always be with you.

Love always,

Werner

Tears rolled down her cheeks and Lotte asked worriedly, "What's wrong? Has something bad happened?"

Honestly, Marlene didn't know.

The radio relieved her from responding, because the RIAS commentator announced, "We have just received the breaking news that Werner Böhm, chief editor of Radio Berlin, has defected and is now speaking to us from the American zone."

Marlene's head snapped in the direction of the radio. "Did I hear this right? He defected?"

"I guess he did," Bruni said with a smug smile.

"And you knew! You met him, didn't you? Why didn't you tell me?" Marlene accused her friend.

"Haven't you sworn to never think of him again?"

If she could, Marlene would have strangled Bruni right there and then, but Lotte interrupted them. "Shush. Don't you want to hear Böhm's speech?"

Of course they did. Glued to the radio, Marlene listened to his sonorous voice explaining the truth about the student leaders and their confessions. With each sentence she grew angrier at the depraved Soviet louts, but at the same time she felt so proud of Werner for finally coming around and speaking the truth.

She didn't know what to think. She had called him a coward and a cruel puppet, had driven him away from her with her constant nagging. Now she regretted her accusations, the burden of guilt creeping into her bones for misjudging him so badly, for not having shown more patience and encouraged him to cut loose from the fetters of his masters.

With his actions he'd taken a terrible risk. The Russians wouldn't sit by idly, but hunt him down, and when they found him, his fate would be a terrible one. She wished she could be with him and comfort him, because he must be terribly afraid.

Once the radio program had ended, the three women were stunned into silence, until Lotte finally said, "Werner Böhm turned out okay after all."

Marlene nodded. "I'm happy for Werner, but sad because I'll probably never see him again."

Then she retreated to her room to weep for Werner, for her impatience, her lack of understanding, and losing him.

***

The next book in the series, On the Brink is about Bruni, who, despite her best intentions, falls in love.

Victor is a simple army engineer, who was deployed to Berlin to build the Tegel airport, when the Russians start choking the city with their blockade.

AUTHOR'S NOTES

Dear Reader,

After finishing the War Girl series that I've been writing for almost three years, it was strange to start a new series. The first book in a series is always the most difficult one, because I don't know the characters yet. Therefore I managed to sneak in a familiar and beloved character, hoping you enjoyed her cameo as much as I did.

As always, I took inspiration from true events, and Werner is loosely modeled after the real-life defector Wolfgang Leonhard. Reading his autobiography, I got a thorough glimpse into the mind of a devoted communist who has to come to terms with the fact that everything he believed in has been perverted and is used to oppress people. I sincerely empathized with tortured Werner as he struggled to align his beliefs with the reality.

Both Georg and Julian are fictional characters, although inspired by the person of Georg Wrazidlo, a doctor and victim of the Nazis and Stalinism. It was he who held the inauguration speech at the Berlin University on 26th of January 1946 and was later arrested under trumped-up antifascist charges because he opposed the Sovietization of the German politics.

Both the American and the Soviet Commandant in Berlin changed several times within the timeline of the book, but I decided to keep a single character for each of them to make it easier to follow the story.

Dean Harris and General Sokolov are each a mish-mash of several real Commandants in Berlin. One of them was Frank L. Howley, whose memoir *Berlin Command* is an eye-opening account of Soviet antics and Western appeasement during a time when the world was sliding into the Cold War. His depictions of the irascible, confrontational and dogmatic personality of his Soviet counterpart Alexander Kotikov were my inspiration for the fictional character of General Sokolov.

While writing *From the Ashes* I've come to love Bruni and her devil-may-care attitude so much, that I decided she'll be the protagonist of the next book in the series, called *On the Brink*.

I don't have a definite release date yet, but if you want to stay informed about upcoming books, sign up for my reader's group here:

https://kummerow.info/subscribe

As always, I want to thank everyone who helped make this book a reality. Daniela Colleo from stunningbookcovers.com made another fantastic cover for me. My editors JJ Toner and Martin O'Hearn polished the manuscript to shine. And my wonderful advance readers pointed out a few more typos for me to fix.

Thank you for reading,

Marion Kummerow

ALSO BY MARION KUMMEROW

Love and Resistance in WW2 Germany

Unrelenting

Unyielding

Unwavering

War Girl Series

Downed over Germany (Prequel)

War Girl Ursula (Book 1)

War Girl Lotte (Book 2)

War Girl Anna (Book 3)

Reluctant Informer (Book 4)

Trouble Brewing (Book 5)

Fatal Encounter (Book 6)

Uncommon Sacrifice (Book 7)

Bitter Tears (Book 8)

Secrets Revealed (Book 9)

Together at Last (Book 10)

Endless Ordeal (Book 11)

Not Without My Sister (Spin-off)

Berlin Fractured

From the Ashes (Book 1)

On the Brink (Book 2)

In the Skies (Book 3)

Into the Unknown (Book 4)

Margarete's Story

Turning Point (Prequel)

A Light in the Window

Historical Romance

Second Chance at First Love

Find all my books here:

http://www.kummerow.info

CONTACT ME

I truly appreciate you taking the time to read (and enjoy) my books. And I'd be thrilled to hear from you!
If you'd like to get in touch with me you can do so via

Twitter:
http://twitter.com/MarionKummerow

Facebook:
http://www.facebook.com/AutorinKummerow

Website
http://www.kummerow.info

Made in United States
Troutdale, OR
06/07/2024

20401621R00148